FURY FROM THE DEEP

To Letty and Oliver with love

DOCTOR WHO
FURY FROM THE DEEP

VICTOR PEMBERTON

Based on the BBC television series by Victor Pemberton by arrangement with the British Broadcasting Corporation

---

No. 110
in the
Doctor Who Library

A TARGET BOOK

published by
the Paperback Division of
W.H. ALLEN & Co. PLC

A Target Book
Published in 1986
By the Paperback Division of
W.H. Allen & Co. PLC
44 Hill Street, London W1X 8LB

First published in Great Britain by
W.H. Allen & Co. PLC 1986

Novelisation copyright © Victor Pemberton, 1986

Original Script copyright © Victor Pemberton, 1968

'Doctor Who' series copyright © British Broadcasting
Corporation, 1968, 1986

The BBC producer of *Fury From The Deep* was Peter Bryant
the director was Hugh David

Typeset in Baskerville by Fleet Graphics, Enfield, Middlesex

Printed and bound in Great Britain by
Anchor Brendon Ltd, Tiptree, Essex

ISBN 0 426 20259 7

This book is sold subject to the condition that it shall not, by way of
trade or otherwise, be lent, resold, hired out or otherwise circulated
without the publisher's prior consent in any form of binding or
cover other than that in which it is published and without a similar
condition including this condition being imposed upon the
subsequent purchaser.

CONTENTS

1	The Deadly Sound	7
2	Something in the Pipeline	16
3	A Pair of White Gloves	31
4	Mr Oak and Mr Quill	41
5	Waiting in the Dark	57
6	The Specimen	69
7	The Figure on the Beach	83
8	The Impeller Shaft	100
9	The Battle of the Giants	119
10	The Spy Within	134
11	The Nerve Centre	151
12	'Scream, Victoria! Scream!'	162

1

The Deadly Sound

The sky had never looked more menacing. Huge clusters of dark grey clouds had overwhelmed the early morning sunshine, threatening the approach of a gathering winter storm. And beneath it all: the sea; the cruel, unyielding sea, crammed with dark secrets that Man on planet Earth has never fully understood. Quiet and calm now, with small white tufts of foam curling gently across the surface, waiting for the gale force winds to lash them into a frenzy. An ancient mariner once said that if you stand alone on the sea shore, you will hear the sound of those who dwell in the deep depths of the ocean. Today was to be just such a day . . .

For the moment, however, the sound was a more familiar one. The TARDIS began to materialise out through the clouds, gradually descending, to hover for a few seconds just above the waves. Finally, it dropped with an undignified flop onto the sea.

A short while later, a small rubber boat was bobbing up and down on the undulating swell, heading its way slowly towards the shore. Inside the boat, three time-travellers were all looking decidedly cold and wet.

'Just like you to land us in the middle of the sea!' Jamie was very disgruntled as he used all his burly strength to row the boat's oars against the outgoing tide.

'Sorry about that.' The Doctor was also rowing energetically, his favourite woollen bobble hat pulled tightly over his ears. 'But don't worry. The TARDIS is perfectly capable of floating.'

Behind them, the TARDIS was swaying gently to and fro on the surface of the water. It was a majestic, if improbable, sight. Passing ships were going to be in for something of a shock when they picked up an old blue police box on their radar scanner.

'Where *exactly* are we?' groaned Victoria. The poor young girl was huddled beneath a large blanket, wearing a thick woollen jumper and skirt, trying to protect herself from the merciless ice-cold breeze. Victoria had never been a good sailor. She had even got sick when her father took her rowing in a boat on the Serpentine Lake in London's Hyde Park. That was back in Victorian times.

The Doctor's eyes were carefully scanning the barren coastline ahead of them. 'Oh, that's England all right. There's no doubt about it.'

'Aye,' grunted Jamie, shivering with the cold. His exposed legs below his kilt had already turned a decided shade of blue. 'W-with this w-weather, it couldna' be anywhere b-but England!'

Although Jamie's comment was a little unjust, the Doctor was probably right. As they approached the coastline they saw that it was, without a doubt, the eastern seaboard of the British Isles. The beach, which was covered entirely with large pebbles, extended for a distance of at least two miles, and perhaps even more. At either end of the beach were enormous steep cliffs, with craggy rocks below, and the entire sea shore was backed by a vast area of sand dunes, which had been shaped into sinister formations by the endless East Anglian winds.

Jamie and the Doctor hauled the rubber boat ashore, then

helped Victoria onto the beach. The Doctor remained at the water's edge for a moment, and gazed out to sea. In one way, he looked a rather comical figure in his woollen bobble hat, shabby old frock coat, and baggy check trousers. But as his eyes scanned the surface of the gently rolling tide, it was obvious he felt uneasy. The Doctor had never really liked the sea. In fact, it was the only thing he really feared. It made him feel insecure, restless.

Jamie was quick to recognise the Doctor's strange mood. He had seen it many times before, always when the Doctor had been anticipating danger. Wandering back to the water's edge, he asked quietly, 'What is it, Doctor?'

The Doctor's eyes were transfixed out towards the sea. 'I don't know, Jamie.' His face was tensed into a frown, as though trying to listen to something. 'There's something not right about this place.'

An ice-cold wind skimmed the surface of the water and swept across the pebbled beach into the sand dunes, sending a funnel of silvery white sand high into the sky. And as the great mist of sand began to settle again, a ghostly, shadowy figure could just be seen, crouched low behind one of the dunes.

The Doctor and his two companions moved on. As they made their way slowly along the beach, their feet made untidy crunching sounds on the rough, hard pebbles. They had only gone a short distance when the Doctor came to an abrupt halt. 'That's curious.' He was staring at something just by his feet.

Victoria wasn't at all concerned. 'It's only foam washed in on the tide. You often find it along the sea shores.'

'Maybe so,' replied the Doctor, bending down to take a closer look at the frothy white substance, 'but there's quite a lot here.'

Victoria turned to look around. The Doctor was right. The entire stretch of the shoreline and beach beyond were covered with large patches of sea foam. It was a very weird sight.

Jamie bent down beside the Doctor. 'D'you think there's something wrong?'

'I'm not sure . . . ' The Doctor scooped up a handful of foam and studied it closely for a moment. 'Here, Jamie – smell.'

Jamie put his nose to the handful of foam. As he did so, the Doctor suddenly slapped it full into Jamie's face.

'Hey!' Jamie was unable to splutter anything more. His face looked as though it was covered in soap suds. The foam also had another curious effect on him, for he immediately burst into a deafening fit of sneezing.

The Doctor and Victoria doubled up with laughter as they watched Jamie, convulsed with sneezing, wiping foam from his face. Jamie's Highland pride was now aroused, and he quickly retaliated by scooping up handfuls of foam and throwing them at the Doctor.

An hilarious foam battle quickly ensued, with the Doctor and Jamie beginning to look like snowmen, their howls of laughter echoing around the beach. The seabirds were not disturbed, because there were no seabirds to be seen. In fact, the sea, the beach, and the cliffs seemed to be deserted of all wild life. But there were other eyes watching the beach, cold and prying eyes . . .

'*Doctor*!'

Victoria's sudden shout brought the fun and games to an abrupt halt. The Doctor and Jamie turned with a start, to find Victoria staring at something in the base of a nearby cliff.

'Don't touch anything!' The Doctor yelled as he ran, with Jamie close behind him.

Victoria had discovered an exposed section of aluminium tube, curling out of the sand and up into the rock face of the cliff. Apart from a few printed figures on the surface of the tube, there were no obvious clues to reveal either its manufacture, or its function.

'What is it, Doctor?' she asked.

The Doctor was tapping the sides of the tube with his

knuckles, trying to decipher the printed figures, which were probably some kind of code. 'Natural gas, Victoria. It's pumped out of the North Sea into this pipeline.'

'Gas from the sea!' Jamie gave the Doctor one of his sceptical Highland looks. After all, he had been brought up in the Scotland of the Jacobean age, long before the arrival of the giant oil and gas sea rigs. 'Who are you tryin' to kid, Doctor?'

'Now, I wonder what that's for?' The Doctor had become keenly interested in a small black box which was fixed to the top of the aluminium tube. 'Jamie, help me up, will you?'

Jamie clasped his hands together, allowing the Doctor to use them as a step to climb up the side of the tube.

Whilst this was going on, Victoria shivered in the cold, and pulled her shawl around her shoulders. She looked all around her, eyes scanning the long stretch of shoreline, and the bleak unfriendliness of the surrounding terrain. Even though Victoria felt tremendous gratitude towards the Doctor for all he had done for her, it was during moments like this that she missed the love and protection of her dear father back in the Victorian age.

The Doctor was now perched cross-legged on top of the aluminium tube. From the inside pocket of his jacket, he took out what looked like his own version of a screwdriver. Slowly, cautiously, he started to open the small black box . . .

At the rear of the beach amongst the sand dunes, the ghostly figure of a man waited patiently. In the distorted, shimmering haze of the early morning, it was almost impossible to see him, lying flat on his stomach, watching the Doctor and his companions through the telescopic sight of his rifle . . .

'What is it, Doctor? Can you see?' Jamie was straining to peer inside the small black box which the Doctor had just opened on top of the aluminium tube. It contained a cluster of micro-chip electronics.

'Looks like some kind of remote-controlled release valve.' The Doctor was prodding at the mass of wires with his screw-

11

driver, causing an immediate flurry of sparks. 'Sure sign we're in the twentieth century. Latter part of it, I'd say.'

Victoria was becoming increasingly nervous. 'Doctor, I do wish you'd hurry. There's something I don't like about this place. It's so – quiet. As though we're being watched.'

The focus gradually cleared through the telescopic sight of the ghostly figure's rifle. It was centred firmly on the Doctor . . .

The Doctor, still perched on top of the aluminium tube, was replacing the small black box he had been looking at.

'Doctor!' Jamie's ear was pressed firmly against the side of the tube. 'I can hear something. A peculiar sound.'

'A sound? Inside the pipeline?' From another of his jacket pockets, the Doctor quickly took out his stethoscope, placed one end of it on the surface of the aluminium tube, and listened to the movement inside.

The sound was definitely there: a deadly sound, slow, rhythmical, thumping, pulsating, like a heartbeat, reverberating along the entire length of the pipeline tube, way out along the depths of the ocean.

Jamie's eyes were glazed with apprehension. He never feared anything he could actually see, but this was an unnatural sound that sent cold shivers up and down his spine. 'What is it, Doctor?' he asked.

'I don't know, Jamie.' The Doctor was grim-faced as he listened to the deadly sound through his stethoscope. The pulsating heartbeat was becoming more mesmeric, more dominant, and the Doctor had that familiar look of sensing impending danger. 'It could be vibration from the pump. Except that . . . ' Suddenly, and without warning, he clutched his shoulder, and yelled out loud in pain. '*Aaah*!'

'Doctor!' Jamie and Victoria watched in horror as the Doctor toppled off the aluminium tube, and slumped with a thud onto the beach.

'Doctor, what is it? What's wrong with you?' Victoria was on her hands and knees in the sand, trying to shake some life back into the Doctor. But the Doctor's body was totally lifeless. His eyes were firmly closed, and his lips had turned a distinct yellow.

Jamie bent down and took hold of the Doctor's hand. It was ice-cold in the chilly wind. Ashen-faced, Jamie raised his eyes to meet Victoria's look of desperation. In a voice trembling with emotion, he said, 'He's dead. The Doctor's dead.'

Victoria wanted to scream out in anguish. But she was too stunned to react in any way at all. For a brief moment she and Jamie just stared at each other in disbelief, tears gradually swelling in her large blue eyes. The Doctor, their friend, their companion – dead. But how could it be possible? The Doctor had survived so many attacks on his life during their travels through time and space. The Doctor was as indestructible as time itself.

Jamie suddenly noticed a small tear in the left-hand corner of the Doctor's jacket. 'He's been shot!' he growled angrily. Rising quickly to his feet, the young Highlander swung his glance around to take in the entire stretch of shoreline. At the top of his voice he yelled, 'Where's the heathen coward that'd shoot a man doon in cold blood!'

Jamie's voice echoed over and over again along the beach, the cliffs, and the sand dunes. If there had been any seagulls riding on the crest of the waves, they would surely have taken flight in panic and terror. But there were no seagulls today, only more and more patches of white sea foam, floating in relentlessly on the swelling tide.

'Will ye no' come out!' Jamie's voice was shaking with emotion and fury. 'Or do I have to come and get ye?'

In the sand dunes at the rear of the beach, Jamie's defiant outline was brought into focus through the telescopic sight of the ghost figure's rifle.

'Murderers!'

It was the last word Jamie spoke. Suddenly, and without warning, he clutched his stomach, crumpled up in pain, and slumped in a heap onto the sand.

'Jamie!' This time Victoria *did* scream. But it was too late.

By the time she reached Jamie, his crumpled body was as lifeless as the Doctor's.

'No! Jamie! No . . .'

Victoria's tears could do nothing to revive the indomitable spirit of the Highland hero. Both he and the Doctor were gone forever, and there was nothing she could do about it. Crouched in the sand alongside Jamie's chilled and stone-like body, Victoria realised she was now completely alone.

The first flurries of snow fluttered down, and began to settle on the two still figures now stretched out on the sand. The air was suddenly quiet. Not a murmur. Not even a light breeze. Victoria, snowflakes glistening in her hair, tears streaming down her flushed cheeks, slowly raised her head.

At first, the sound was barely audible. But there was no mistaking it was there. The same, slow, rhythmical, pulsating sound like a heartbeat which the Doctor had heard reverberating inside the pipeline tube.

Victoria sprang to her feet with a start. The beach was no longer deserted. Standing in the dunes a short distance away, was the towering figure of a man, wearing a shiny black uniform and helmet. In his hand he held the telescopic rifle which had brought down both the Doctor and Jamie. Soon, other figures were beginning to emerge from the mist: sinister figures, all in black uniforms and helmets.

'Who are you?' Victoria's voice, trembling with fear and anger, screeched and echoed across the beach. 'Why are you doing this to us?'

The sinister figures in black remained silent. Then they were joined by two odd-looking men, one tall and thin, the other small and fat. Both were wearing white medical tunics and caps.

Victoria's immediate instinct was to run. But as she turned, she was confronted by a sight of sheer horror. The beach all around her was a mass of white sea foam. And out of the foam appeared large clumps of seaweed, all pulsating with life, like a human heart.

'*No!*' Victoria's scream provoked the most chilling

14

response from the seaweed clumps, for they suddenly burst into a frenzied cacophony of sound, pulsating faster and faster, as if daring the intruder to move towards them.

Victoria covered her ears, desperately trying to protect them from the deafening, deadly sound.

In the sand dunes, the towering, ghostly figure raised his rifle, and focussed on Victoria through the telescopic sight.

As soon as she was struck down by the silent bullet, Victoria's cry of pain was muffled by the pulsating sound of the seaweed clumps in the foam all around her.

And then it was quiet again. Not a murmur. Not even a slight breeze.

The sinister figures in the dunes watched and waited. One by one, the clumps of seaweed withdrew into the safety of the foam.

The snow was falling thick and fast now, leaving a thin carpet of white over beach and cliffs.

It took only a few minutes for snowflakes to cover the three lifeless bodies spread-eagled forlornly in the sand.

2

Something in the Pipeline

The darkness seemed interminable. No dreams, not even a nightmare. Just a long, dark void.

Victoria was the first to stir. Her eyes suddenly sprang open, to be greeted by a strange vapour-like mist. She tried to move her lips in an effort to speak. But all she could manage was a croak. Somehow she felt disconnected from the rest of her body, because she was unable to move any part of it. Finally, she made another attempt to speak.

'Doc-tor . . . Doc-tor . . . '

Although her voice was barely audible, it was enough to produce an immediate response from the Doctor, who was somewhere very close by.

'Victoria! Are you . . . all right?' He spoke in a strangulated voice, as if the words were stuck in his throat.

'I . . . I can't move . . . my legs . . . '

'I can't move . . . either . . . ' Jamie's voice joined them, also from close by. He sounded like his tongue had become too large for his mouth. 'Wh – what's happened to us?'

One thing was clear. The three time-travellers were certainly not dead, and they were no longer on the beach. They were lying flat on their backs, head to head, spread-

16

eagled on the floor of some enormous building, which at the present moment appeared to them as nothing more than a blurred haze. And all around them, odd sounds. Bleeping, pumping, thumping, electrical, mechanical.

Gradually, the haze began to clear. Two blurred shadowy figures were standing over the trio, each carrying telescopic rifles. The Doctor managed to focus on them, and regain some of the strength in his voice.

'Would you mind telling us where we are?'

The two blurred figures remained silent, and bent down to take a closer look. Their faces seemed large and oval, grotesque and distorted.

'Why don't you answer?'

Once again Victoria tried to move, but without success. 'Doctor, what have they done to us?' she wailed. Even the ability to cry had been denied her. 'I can't move!'

The Doctor tried rolling the pupils of his eyes, but they felt too heavy and stiff. 'Don't panic, Victoria. I think we've been tranquillised.'

'What!' Jamie was outraged. 'Who do they think they are?'

'I think it's we who should be asking the questions.' A third face joined the two blurred figures. The voice was gruff and bronchial. 'And I shall expect quite a lot of answers.'

The haze had now completely cleared to reveal a burly-looking man, probably in his early fifties, with greying hair, a jutting jaw, and vacant grey eyes. With a wave of his hand, he dismissed the two guards, and studied each of the three helpless figures spread-eagled before him.

Jamie found it agonising to try and move the muscles in his face. 'What is this place?' he croaked.

The man with the jutting jaw leaned closer, enabling Jamie to read the large name-patch on his shiny black plastic uniform: *ROBSON, S. CONTROLLER 1*. 'You mean you don't know?' said Robson, the corner of his mouth curling into a cynical smile.

Jamie glared at the jutting jaw with frustrated anger. 'If I could just get up . . . ' he snarled through clenched teeth.

'I shouldn't try if I were you!' Robson's smile quickly faded.

'You know, lying in this position, it *is* rather difficult to communicate,' said the Doctor. He was right. He and his two companions did look faintly ridiculous stretched out in such an undignified position on the floor.

'Shall we give them some U4, sir?' The voice was that of a young man in his late twenties. He was a weak-looking individual, with blue eyes, a pale face and gaunt expression, and a mop of blond, unruly hair that constantly flopped carelessly over his right eye. His uniform was too big for him, and he looked as though he could do with a good meal. He had a cultured way of speaking, which was in complete contrast to his boss, Robson. His name-patch showed: *HARRIS, F. CONTROLLER 2.*

For a moment, Robson ignored his second-in-command. He was too occupied staring menacingly into Jamie's eyes.

Harris tried again. 'Mr Robson, sir. The U4.'

This time Robson swung an irritated glance at him, as if to refuse the request. But after quickly thinking better of it, he straightened up, waved his hand, and strutted off.

Harris immediately signalled two engineers to come forward. They were carrying small transparent gas cylinders with mouth-piece attachments. Harris took one of the cylinders, then all three engineers knelt down beside the Doctor, Jamie, and Victoria.

'What are you going to do?' Victoria's eyes rolled from side to side in helpless panic, as Harris approached her with the cylinder mouth-piece. 'Keep away from me . . . no!'

'It's all right, don't worry,' said Harris, flicking a lock of his unruly hair out of his eye. 'The U4 will soon bring you round.'

'No!' Victoria's terrified yell of protest was instantly stifled by the mouth-piece. The same treatment was also given to the Doctor and Jamie, and the sound of hissing gas was heard immediately.

It took just sixty seconds for the U4 to achieve its task. The first to feel its effect was Jamie, who suddenly felt life returning to his big toes. He quickly pushed off the mouthpiece, sat up, and yelled out triumphantly. 'I can move!'

Seconds later, the Doctor and Victoria were also revived, and all three were soon on their feet again. At last, they were able to look around the extraordinary building they had been brought to. It was indeed a remarkable sight.

They were standing in what seemed to be some kind of Communications Control Hall, the nerve-centre of a huge gas refinery. The Hall was completely circular, like the inside of a mosque, and it looked as though it had been built entirely of aluminium and perspex. The floor of the Hall was in fact a well, flanked all the way around by a narrow observation platform, which was reached by means of two or three perspex steps. The walls themselves were almost completely covered by a mass complex of snake-like pressure tubes, valves, gauges, wheels, handles and levers. The windows were port-holes, placed at high angles to reveal nothing but the open sky.

Dominating the Control Hall itself, however, was the massive aluminium pipeline, which curled overhead around the walls, out to the beach, and beyond, to the rigs in the North Sea. On the observation platform there was a transparent door, through which could be seen the Impeller Area. Here the giant piston thumped up and down relentlessly twenty-four hours a day, pumping natural gas through the main pipeline, out to receiving stations in Southern England.

The main communications panel was a towering triangular shaped cone in the centre of the Hall. The cone contained at least ten video monitors, and a vast array of satellite computer systems, all linking the Refinery to its rigs and the outside world. And set on top of the cone was a huge illuminated panel, showing the actual position of the rigs out at sea, indicated by flashing coloured lights.

The Control Hall was manned by a team of engineers and communication technicians, each of them wearing identical one-piece uniforms made of a shiny black plastic material with patches showing each crewman's name and job grading. Only the engineers wore helmets, and these were made out of reinforced transparent perspex.

The Doctor, Jamie, and Victoria stared in wonder at the vast complex of computerised equipment surrounding them. Lights flashing, buzzers buzzing, distorted voices calling from video monitors, sinister figures in black dashing back and forth in frenzied activity. And behind this, the constant throbbing sound of the giant piston pump, reverberating around the metallic walls.

'You were on the beach by the pipeline in a restricted area! Why?' The Doctor, Victoria, and Jamie turned with a start as Robson's coarse voice cut through the atmosphere like a rifle shot. Robson was a crude man: there was no place in his life for moderation.

'We were lost, that's all,' said Victoria timidly.

Robson ignored her. His attention was fixed firmly on the Doctor. 'You were seen tampering with the emergency release valve remote controls. You're a saboteur!'

'He's no such thing!' Victoria suddenly regained her fiery spirit. 'He's a Doctor – well, sort of . . .'

The Doctor's face creased up into its usual affable, innocent smile. 'I can assure you, sir, I was merely being inquisitive.'

Harris tried to be logical. 'Mr Robson, I don't really see how these people could've had anything to do with . . .'

'When I want your opinion, Harris, I'll ask for it!' Robson's eyes were bulging with anger. It was perfectly obvious there was no love lost between the Chief Engineer and his second-in-command. In fact, Robson had always resented the fact that a young man had been appointed to the job, and straight out of University at that. 'Lock them up in one of the cabins. I'll interrogate them later!'

As he turned, Robson discovered a group of engineers

watching him. 'What are you lot standing around for!' he yelled, pushing his way past them. 'When are we going to get some work done around here?' The engineers scattered, and hurried back to their jobs.

Jamie watched Robson go, then turned to Harris and asked scornfully, 'Is he always as charming as that?'

Harris was clearly embarrassed by his chief's behaviour. 'Well, we've something of an emergency on at the moment. The fact is, we've just lost contact with one of our rigs out at sea.'

The Doctor was immediately curious. 'You mean, your communications system has broken down?'

'No. It's just that the crew aren't answering.'

This made Victoria indignant. 'Well, you can't blame us for that!'

Harris was unconsciously biting his upper lip. 'There's also been a drop in pressure in the feed line from the rigs,' he said. Then he turned to the Doctor with a reproving, suspicious look. 'You were seen tampering with a release valve on the pipeline.'

Now it was Jamie's turn to be angry. 'That's no reason for shooting us down like animals!' His outburst provoked the two armed guards into moving in closer.

Harris shrugged his shoulders. 'I'm sorry about that, but you must realise we're under a security alert and . . . ' he sighed apologetically, 'I'm afraid I'll have to do as Mr Robson says, and lock you up. Follow me, please.'

Harris moved off, followed by Victoria. For a moment, Jamie stubbornly refused to budge, but after a pacifying look from the Doctor, he joined the others, closely followed by the two armed guards.

As they left, a buzzing sound was heard, and a green light started flashing excitedly at the top of the Control Cone.

A young woman approached the Guard Room at the main entrance of the Refinery. She looked as though she was in her late twenties, but could have been a little older. Harris's wife, Maggie, was a beautiful woman, in a very English way. But her peach-like complexion, dark brunette hair, and strongly defined features, disguised a firm and determined nature. Maggie was the kind of woman Harris needed for a wife.

'Have you a pass, please, madam?' The guard on duty made it quite clear that no unauthorised person was going to get past him today.

'Pass?'

'We have instructions that no-one is to leave or enter the Compound without a written pass from Chief Robson. Not until after the emergency.'

Maggie was indignant. She knew something odd was going on at the Refinery today, but this was downright ludicrous. 'But you know who I am,' she said. The guard shrugged his shoulders. Maggie stiffened. 'My husband is second-in-command to Chief Robson.'

'I'm aware of that, Mrs Harris.'

'Then let me pass, please.' Maggie stepped forward as if to walk straight past the barrier. To her absolute astonishment, she found the end of an automatic rifle barrel pointing straight at her chest.

The guard stared hard into Maggie's eyes, making it perfectly obvious that he was taking his job seriously. In a polite, but firm voice, he said, 'I'm sorry, madam. I think you should return to the residential block.'

For a brief moment, Maggie stared back in disbelief at the guard. But in that split second, she had decided that it is never wise to argue with a loaded automatic rifle. She turned haughtily, and swept off towards the compound area. Only one thing was now uppermost in her mind. Something very odd was indeed going on at the Refinery today.

'A movement in the pipeline? Impossible!' Harris was doing his best to show that he wasn't at all concerned. 'Marine life couldn't possibly get inside the pipeline tube. It would never get past the drilling pumps.'

'Aye. Well, be that as it may,' said Jamie, sitting cross-legged on the top bunk, 'but there *was* something in that tube, because I heard it too!'

'And so did I,' said Victoria from the lower bunk.

Harris had brought the Doctor and his companions to one of the crew cabins in the Control Compound. It was a small, confined space, with two bunk beds, a wash basin, small desk, wardrobe, and a ventilator shaft in the wall measuring about four or five feet. It was more like a prison cell.

'If the pressure is down in the pipeline, perhaps this is the reason why.' The Doctor was staring out through the port-hole window, towards the beach and open sea. 'Marine life has managed to find a way into the tube.'

'Impossible!' replied Harris. 'We've spent years of time, money, and research perfecting our emergency systems.'

The Doctor smiled wryly. 'Well, perhaps there's a fracture somewhere along your pipeline, and something's got in that way?'

Harris had his doubts. And he was shocked when the Doctor suggested that they turn off the gas flow, at least until they'd had the chance to find out if there really was a movement in the pipeline. Harris insisted that Chief Robson would never agree to that.

'Why not?' said the Doctor, turning from the window.

Harris lowered his eyes awkwardly. 'Mr Robson prides himself that the flow has never been shut off since he took charge. He doesn't believe in working to the book.'

The Doctor shook his head with a sigh. 'Then he's a very silly man.'

'Maybe so,' replied Harris, astutely, 'but he appears to be right about one thing.' He brushed his usual lock of hair from his eye. 'You do seem to know quite a lot about what we're doing here.'

Mick Carney's face was on one of the video monitors at the Control Cone. Carney had been in charge of the off-shore

23

drilling Rig D for the past nine months, and had increased gas flow production by nearly four percent.

'Carney! What the hell's going on out there?' Robson was yelling out his frustration at the video monitor. For the past few hours, contact had been lost with Rig D, throwing the Refinery's communication network into disarray.

'Everything's quite all right, Mr Robson,' Carney's voice was calm and barely audible. Although he was a man only in his mid-thirties, his appearance had visibly changed during the past twenty-four hours. His face was white, eyes sunken, and hair flecked with grey streaks. 'We have the situation under control, sir.'

'What? What did you say?' Robson was straining to hear Carney's faint voice. 'Speak up man! I can't hear a word you're saying!'

Carney merely smiled back without saying a word. He had a strange look in his eyes.

Robson turned quickly to David Price, the video operator. 'What's wrong with this thing? Are we losing volume?'

'No, sir. It's nothing to do with us. I don't understand it.' Price adjusted the controls, and spoke louder towards the monitor. 'Mr Carney, could you speak a little louder, please?'

'Everything . . . is under control . . . ' Carney's voice was quite lifeless, almost as though he was day-dreaming.

Robson snapped back impatiently. 'What about the emergency crew we sent out to you? Have they arrived yet?'

'They must stay here now . . . stay here . . . '

'Do what?' Robson leaned forward, squinted at the monitor.

'Accident . . . slight accident . . . ' Carney's voice was now no more than a whisper. 'Two men . . . out of action . . . '

For a brief moment, the frenzied activity in the Control Hall came to an abrupt halt. All eyes were turned towards the video monitor.

Robson's patience finally cracked. 'Now you listen to me, Carney. I want that rig back into working operation right away!' And raising his voice to a shout: 'Do you hear me, Carney!'

Carney's face remained impassive, his eyes showing no sign of life. All he could be heard mumbling was, ' . . . control . . . everything . . . under control . . . '

'Carney! Carney!'

Even as Robson was yelling out, Carney's voice faded, and the video picture started to break up. Suddenly, the screen was blank.

'Come in, Rig D. Come in, please!' Price was anxiously adjusting every control switch he could lay his hands on. 'I think we've lost contact again, sir!'

'Well, fix it, man!' Robson turned angrily from the Control Cone, to find himself face-to-face with Harris.

'Mr Robson, I think we should turn off the gas flow coming in from the rigs, and make a check,' he suggested.

If looks could kill, Robson would have been responsible for Harris's instant death. 'You think *what*, Mr Harris?'

Harris took a deep breath. 'That Doctor chap – the stranger – he said he heard a movement coming from inside the pipeline on the beach.'

'Oh, did he now?' replied Robson cynically, his jutting jaw more protruding than ever. 'And did he say what he thought it was? Mice?'

'Mr Robson!' The chief engineer, sweat streaming down his face, was calling from the open door of the Impeller Area. 'She's down another three. Pressure's just on one-fifty-seven.'

Robson called back. He was clearly shocked. 'One-fifty-seven! Are you sure?'

'Absolutely, sir.'

Harris quickly followed Robson towards the Impeller Area. 'That means pressure is down at the rate of three thousand cubic feet every . . . ' he checked his watch, '. . . every twenty minutes. This definitely proves that something *is* blocking the pipeline.'

'It proves nothing of the sort.' Robson had reached the

steps leading up to the observation platform. 'If anything, it's a faulty gauge.'

'At least give us the benefit of the doubt,' pleaded Harris. 'Let's check the inside of that pipeline.'

Robson turned suddenly. The veins in his forehead were swelling out in anger. 'For the last time Mr Harris – no!'

'Mr Robson, listen to me!' For once, Harris was determined to be heard. 'This all ties up with what I've been trying to tell you. For three weeks now there's been a regular and increasing build-up and fall in pressure. The time ratios correspond to form a definite progressive pattern.'

'Statistics! Always statistics!'

Harris persisted. 'At least look at my calculations.'

'All right! All right!' Robson's patience was running out fast. 'Go and get your stupid bits of paper, and I'll show you where you've gone wrong!'

Harris rushed across to his desk to collect the file he was referring to. His briefcase was lying on top of the desk. He quickly opened it, and felt inside. His shock was immediate. 'It's gone!' He turned, calling back to Robson who was watching him from the observation platform. 'The file – it's gone!'

There was a knowing look on Robson's face. 'Well, well, well, has it now?'

Harris was desperately tipping out the contents of his briefcase onto the desk. Some pencils, a newspaper, and a portable sonic calculator. But no file. 'I'm sure I put it in here this morning. I must have left the file in my desk at home.' He started to move off. 'I'll go and get it . . .'

'You stay right where you are, Harris!' Robson's bronchial voice echoed across the Control Hall. 'I'm not doing your job here as well as my own!'

Harris glared back defiantly. 'What's the matter, sir? Are you afraid I might prove you wrong?'

Robson couldn't believe his ears. This was the first time anyone in the Refinery had dared to challenge him about anything. And this, coming from a young upstart straight out of a red-brick University. He was about to yell back at Harris when he suddenly realised the entire Control Hall crew were watching him. He strolled back casually to Harris, stared him straight in the eyes and said quietly, 'All right, boy. Go and get your little pieces of paper. But you'd better have something more than a high-flown theory to show me. Because if you haven't, I'm going to kick you right back into that University – where you belong!'

In the crew cabin, Jamie was perched perilously on the Doctor's shoulders, peering out through a small metal grille above the door.

'See anything?' The Doctor called in a hushed voice.

Jamie looked along the corridor outside, then whispered back down to the Doctor, 'All clear.' He started to pull out the metal grille.

'Don't bother, Jamie,' called Victoria. 'I can do it with this.' She took a hairpin from her hair, and held it up for Jamie to see.

'Och! Don't be so stupid! Ye canna pick a door lock with a hairpin.'

The Doctor squirmed as he took the weight of Jamie on his shoulders. Suddenly, there was a loud bang as Jamie pulled out the metal grille, and accidentally dropped it to the floor.

'Clumsy!' Victoria had her fingers in her ears.

Jamie glared at her, then struggled to pull himself through the very narrow opening left by the grille. Victoria ignored him, and started to tackle the door lock with her hairpin.

In the corridor outside, Jamie was half-way through the opening above the crew cabin door. Although agile, he did, in fact, look very clumsy as he tried to pull himself through the narrow opening. Suddenly, he froze. Someone was coming along the corridor. He quickly closed his eyes, hoping he wouldn't be noticed.

Maggie Harris approached, just in time to see her husband coming down the corridor in the opposite direction. To Jamie's horror, they stopped to talk just below him.

'Maggie! Where've you been? I've been trying to contact you.' Harris was on edge after his exchange with Robson.

'I was going into the village, but Robson's clamped down on security.' Maggie's hair was windblown from the rough weather outside. 'I was on my way to see you to get a pass.'

'Yes. There's been a bit of a flap on!'

'Well, can you get me a pass?'

'At the moment – not a hope. Now, listen carefully, Maggie. I want you to do something for me!'

Jamie strained to hear what Harris was saying.

'There's a file – it's probably in the top drawer of my desk in the study. Could you go and get it, and bring it to me here?'

Maggie agreed, but looked puzzled. 'What's the panic?' she said.

'I'll explain later. Fast as you can!'

Harris was gone before Maggie had a chance to answer. She paused, just long enough to watch him disappear along the corridor, then hurried off back the same way she came.

Jamie breathed a sigh of relief, then indicated for the Doctor to push him through.

Inside the crew cabin, the Doctor and Victoria were looking up at Jamie's dangling feet.

'He's stuck!' Victoria giggled, and went back to work on the door lock with her hairpin.

'Hold on, Jamie!' called the Doctor, finding a stool to stand on. 'Here we go!' He grabbed hold of Jamie's feet, and gave them one final push.

In the corridor outside, Jamie fell with a thud to the floor.

'I told you not to bother!' Jamie looked up to find Victoria standing over him, smugly putting the hairpin back into her hair.

The Doctor came out of the crew cabin. 'Sorry about that, Jamie.' He and Victoria had broad grins on their faces as they hurried off down the corridor. Jamie glared at them, then followed.

Harris's apartment was one of many scattered around the Refinery Compound and was some distance from most of the other married quarters. There was nothing luxurious about the apartment. It was functional, with most of the furniture made out of the same transparent perspex material used in the Refinery. There were four main rooms: a lounge/diner, kitchen, bedroom, and study. Maggie's one personal touch was the various tropical plants creeping up the walls, some of them looking like prehistoric creatures attempting to take over the place. But the harsh East Anglian winds were not hospitable to the tropical immigrants, and their survival during the winter months depended wholly on the constant flow of gas central heating.

Maggie's hair was glistening with snowflakes as she hurried in, and used all her strength to close the front door against the biting gale-force wind outside. Then she turned, and quickly made her way to the study.

Maggie went straight to Harris's desk. It was, as usual, cluttered with papers and books. 'Top drawer,' she said to herself, opening the drawer and searching it: Nothing there except stationery and technical photographs. Then she searched the other two drawers. The same.

Just as she was about to give up the search, Maggie caught a glimpse of the file Harris had asked her for. It was partly submerged beneath the papers on top of the desk. She started clearing the papers, but suddenly stopped with a shocked start. Something was spread out on top of the file.

It was a small clump of seaweed.

Maggie couldn't believe her eyes. What was such a thing doing inside the apartment? Wet and slimy, pitted with bubbles and streaked with veins, the intruder was the last thing Maggie expected to find sitting on top of a file on her husband's desk. She took a closer look. 'Where the hell did you come from?' she said, as if expecting a reply. The seaweed clump was glistening beneath the glare of the desk lamp. Maggie sighed. 'Ah well. Out you go . . . ' She put her hand out to remove the clump. In one swift, terrifying

29

movement, the seaweed clump suddenly sprang to life, wrapped itself around Maggie's hand, then dropped to the floor. Maggie screamed out in agony, as though stung by a bee or wasp.

For a moment, Maggie just stood there, shaking with fright, clutching her injured hand, staring in disbelief at the now lifeless seaweed clump on the floor. Then, in one angry impetuous movement, she quickly picked up the seaweed, rushed into the kitchen with it, and frantically threw it out the back door.

The Harris's verandah outside the kitchen was protected from the snow by a slanting perspex roof and wind-breakers. Pots of winter-flowering shrubs were surviving the extreme cold, but not so the concrete floor which had been cracked by the endless hard frosts. The seaweed clump was on that floor now, where Maggie had thrown it. It seemed out of place there: wet, slimy, and ominously still.

Then there came a thumping, heartbeat sound. The bubbles on the surface of the seaweed clump started to pop, followed by a hissing sound: the sound of escaping gas . . .

3

A Pair of White Gloves

Pieter van Lutyens had never liked Controller Robson, not from the first day he set eyes on him. The Dutchman had always found Robson to be arrogant, opinionated, and thoroughly ruthless to his crewmen. Two years ago, van Lutyens had been appointed by his government to serve as a technical adviser to the Refinery, at the request of the British Euro-Gas Corporation. He was a likeable little man, dumpy, balding, quick-witted, the very personification of someone who has learnt how to get on well with people. With most people that is – except Robson.

'Van Lutyens, are you trying to tell me how to do my job?' Robson was glaring again. He was on the observation platform in the Control Hall, checking out computer flow levels.

'Mr Robson,' van Lutyens spoke English with no trace of an accent, 'the morale of the men out on those rigs is extremely low. We've got to do something about it!'

'I make the decisions around here, my friend – not you!' Robson turned his back on the Dutchman and continued what he was doing.

Van Lutyens refused to be ignored. He gripped the platform hand rail, and called up to Robson. 'You don't understand! I've just come back from the Control Rig. The men are behaving strangely. They are being affected by something out there in the sea.'

'You're here to advise me on any technical problems, not to spread alarm amongst my crews,' retorted Robson.

Van Lutyens was gripping the hand rail so tightly that his knuckles were turning white. 'Why won't you ever listen to the facts?'

Robson swung around angrily. 'Now you listen to me, van Lutyens. It was Megan Jones and those fools on the Board who sent you here. I told them it would never work. And it hasn't!'

'Only because you are too proud to accept advice.'

'Let's get something straight, my friend.' Robson pointed his finger menacingly at van Lutyens. 'When I need your advice, I'll ask for it!'

Van Lutyens managed a wry smile. 'By then it will be too late.'

Just above where Robson and van Lutyens were having their tense exchange, three faces appeared at an upper corridor window overlooking the Control Hall. It was the Doctor, Jamie, and Victoria. Slowly, quietly, they eased open the window. As they did so, there was a flurry of activity at the Communications Cone.

'Mr Robson!' Price's voice boomed out above the deafening thumping sound of the giant impeller. 'I've got Chief Baxter at Control Rig, sir. He's on Video Three.'

Robson immediately broke away from van Lutyens, and hurried across to the Cone. Chief Baxter's face was on the Video Three monitor. He looked tired and strained.

'Yes, Baxter? What is it?'

Baxter was one of the most experienced drilling engineers in the North Sea gas fields. Now a man in his late fifties, he was once tipped to take on the job that eventually went to Robson. But Baxter was too vital to the off-shore drilling exploration programme, so he was given command of the Control Rig.

'Has Mr van Lutyens arrived yet, sir?'

'Yes, he's here!' snapped Robson. 'Why?'

Baxter coughed slightly. It was just a dry cough, more a clearing of the throat. But it was noticeable. 'He's told you then, sir? I mean – about how the men feel out here?'

'Look, Baxter – I'm running this outfit, not Mr van Lutyens. You take your orders from me!'

'Yes I know sir, but – ' he coughed again, 'there's something else.' As he spoke now, there were signs of breathlessness. 'Something . . . seems to have got inside the pipeline.'

Everyone in the Control Hall stopped what they were doing. All eyes were turned towards the Video Three monitor.

Robson squinted at the monitor screen, as though he was short-sighted. 'What the hell are you talking about, man?'

There were beads of sweat on Baxter's forehead. He dabbed it with his handkerchief. 'I know it sounds ridiculous, sir. But whatever it is, it's in the tubes feeding in from the other rigs. We've all heard it.'

Van Lutyens had now joined Robson, staring anxiously at the screen. 'Heard?' said Robson. 'Heard what?'

'This sound . . . ' Baxter's voice was becoming more and more breathless. 'At first . . . I thought it was something to do with the pumps. But . . . it isn't. It's a . . . peculiar sound . . . a sort of regular thumping . . . pulsating.' For a split second it seemed that he held his breath, then said, 'It's like listening to the sound of your own heartbeat.'

'That's it!' said the Doctor in his hidden vantage point. He rubbed his hands together excitedly. 'That's exactly what I heard in the pipeline down on the beach.'

Victoria bit her lip nervously. 'Yes, Doctor, but what *is* that sound?'

The Doctor's exuberance quickly subsided. 'I don't know, Victoria. But we're going to find out. Come on, Jamie!'

Jamie was perplexed. 'Where're we going?'

'I want to take another look at that pipeline.'

The Doctor and Jamie left the window, and started to move off down the corridor. As they did so, Victoria tagged on behind. But the Doctor stopped suddenly, and turned. 'Er – no, Victoria. Not you.'

Victoria looked hurt. 'Oh – why not?'

'Not the sort of job for a young girl,' said the Doctor. And when Victoria was about to object, he merely had to smile at her like a protective uncle and say, 'Better go back and wait in the crew cabin. We shan't be long. Please?'

As usual, the Doctor won Victoria over, and she reluctantly made her way back to the cabin. As soon as the Doctor and Jamie were out of sight however, she sneaked off down another corridor to do a little snooping of her own.

In the bedroom of the Harris's apartment, Maggie was not feeling at all well. Her hand was swelling up from the sting she had received from the seaweed clump, and she began to feel drowsy and disoriented. Sitting on the edge of the bed, she closed her eyes, rubbed them, then opened them again. She looked around her. Everything seemed to be just very slightly out of focus.

The room was suddenly flooded by a burst of sunshine. Maggie gradually eased herself up from the bed, steadied herself, and went to the window.

The snow had stopped falling, and that which had settled was beginning to thaw. But the sky was still a relentless sheet of dark grey, relieved only by an unexpected chink of sunlight. Maggie looked up and felt the brief caress of warmth on her cheeks. But the glare was too much, so she quickly shielded her eyes with one hand, and left the room.

By the time she reached the kitchen, Maggie was feeling very shaky indeed. She made straight for the internal communications video, set in the wall above the dishwasher, then, using the remote control transmitter, tapped out three numbers. Almost immediately, Price's face appeared on the monitor screen. 'Control!'

Cold beads of sweat were pouring down Maggie's face, and she found it hard to speak: 'M - Mrs Harris. Married Q - Quarters Block 420. Is m - my husband there p-please?'

'We have an emergency on here at the moment, Mrs Harris. Is anything wrong?' asked Price.

'C-could you please f-find him. Tell him . . . tell him I'm not feeling very well.'

'Right away, Mrs Harris!' Price's face disappeared from the monitor screen.

Maggie found her way to a chair at the kitchen table by the back door. Her head was now throbbing with pain. As she sat there, her mind became restless and confused. She could hear voices, all talking together at the same time. Dozens of them. Hundreds.

Suddenly, she looked up with a start. The voices had gone, to be replaced immediately by another, more positive sound. Thumping. Pulsating. Maggie's eyes were rivetted towards the back door. The thumping sound was becoming louder, and louder. It was like listening to the sound of her own heartbeat . . .

At the Refinery, someone was moving around in the darkness of the Oyxgen Store Room. He was tall and thin, and was clothed from head to foot in a white tunic, trousers, cap, and gloves. Only the face of the mysterious figure could not be seen. It was hidden behind a rubber gas mask.

Slowly, methodically, the white gloved hands felt their way along the rows of emergency oxygen cylinders. Finally, they selected one, broke the seal on the cylinder cap, and turned on the tap. Immediately, a hissing sound was heard. White gloves moved on, then did the same with two other cylinders. Gradually, the hissing sound increased.

Suddenly, the masked figure turned in alarm towards the door.

Victoria was snooping around the corridor outside. She tried the handle of a door marked *LABORATORY* 2. It was locked. She turned with a start. Footsteps were approaching the far end of the corridor. She looked around frantically for the quickest means of escape. On the opposite side of the corridor was a door marked *OXYGEN EMERGENCY SUPPLY*. She tried the handle and the door opened. She rushed in. As she did so, Harris came hurrying down the corridor.

Inside the Oyxgen Store Room, Victoria listened at the door. The sound of Harris's footsteps outside gradually disappeared. Victoria breathed a sigh of relief.

As she was about to leave the room, Victoria heard the hissing sound of escaping oxygen. She tried to turn on the light, but it wasn't working. The fumes started to make her cough a little, so she covered her mouth with one hand. Then she quickly felt her way around in the dark, searching the racks of cylinders to find out where the escaping gas was coming from. Within a moment or so, she had managed to turn off all the taps.

The room was now silent again, and Victoria began to recover from the overpowering atmosphere. It was only then that she realised she was not alone. She slowly looked around, her eyes desperately trying to penetrate the eerie darkness of the room.

'Who's there?' Her voice was no more than a timid whisper.

Suddenly, a shaft of light from the corridor outside, beamed straight onto Victoria's face. Standing in the open doorway was the sinister gas-masked figure. Victoria made a rush for the door, only to find it slammed closed before she could get there. She frantically tried turning the handle, but in the corridor outside, a pair of white-gloved hands turned the key in the lock of the Oyxgen Room door.

'Let me out of here!' yelled Victoria, struggling to open the door. But the door was very firmly locked, and once again she was a prisoner. For a moment, she just stood there in the dark, alone and frightened. Then she quickly took the hairpin from her hair, and set to work on the door lock.

By this time, white-gloved hands in the corridor outside were poised over a wall unit which controlled temperature and ventilation inside the Oyxgen Room. Across the unit were printed the words: *EMERGENCY VENTILATOR*. White-gloved hands turned the dial switch to *OPEN*.

Victoria turned with a start. There was an electronic hum coming from somewhere behind her in the dark. Instinctively, she fumbled for the light switch on the wall, and, to her surprise, this time it came on. Her attention was immediately focussed to the other side of the room. The flaps of a huge ventilator grill were sliding open.

The electronic hum continued for what seemed like an eternity. Victoria's nerve was beginning to break, and she started tapping gently on the door. 'Hallo!' she called, hardly daring to raise her voice. 'Is anyone there? For goodness sake, where is everybody?'

As she spoke, the electronic hum came to an abrupt halt.

In the few moments of silence that followed, Victoria, face pressed up against the door, closed her eyes, hoping that what was happening to her was nothing but a terrible dream. Or was it a nightmare? Her heart was pounding, thumping. At least, that's what she thought she could hear. But the sound was becoming too loud, too intense. And then suddenly, there was another sound – a hissing and popping. Victoria's eyes sprang open, and she gasped with horror. On the other side of the room, a vast mass of white sea foam was bursting through the ventilator grille. And while Victoria looked on helplessly, something began to emerge from the foam . . .

The Doctor and Jamie had found their way to the Impeller Area. The place was deserted, but, by peering through a transparent connecting door, they could see Robson, van Lutyens, and the crew, all working in a tense atmosphere in the Control Hall. The noise from the giant impeller was deafening, so the Doctor signalled to Jamie to follow him through another transparent door, this one marked: *PIPELINE ROOM*.

The Doctor peered around the door. No-one there. He entered cautiously, with Jamie close behind. The room they were now in was large and rectangular in shape, with a complex of vertical pressure tubes running up the walls. And once again there were ventilator grilles everywhere, including one enormous grille cut into the wall in a far corner of the room.

Jamie was immediately interested in a huge section of transparent pipeline, which curved down from the ceiling and disappeared into the floor. 'Is this the pipeline?' he said.

'Yes, part of it.' The Doctor climbed up two steps to the observation platform. 'All these pipes are a continuation of the pipeline we found on the beach.'

'Aye. But you can see inside that bit.'

The Doctor was taking a close look at the pipeline tube section. He breathed on it, rubbed it with his coat-sleeve, then peered inside. 'The transparent part is for checking for condensation,' he said. Then he turned to Jamie with a wry grin. 'And anything else that might get inside . . .'

In the Oyxgen Room, Victoria was too chilled with terror to call for help. Her eyes were transfixed on the ventilator grille, where the tendrils of an enormous seaweed creature were rising up out of the mass of white foam, which was now gushing into the room.

The weed creature had no shape or form. There seemed to be no head or eyes or mouth, no features of any kind to compare it with any known form of marine life. This was a living algae, grown to mammoth proportions, hissing and popping, slithering its way through the ventilator grille, into the very heart of the Refinery itself.

Victoria, cowering against the door, was finding it difficult to breathe. The atmosphere was stifling. She started to cough. Finally, in desperation, she started thumping on the the door as loud as she could.

'Let me out!' she yelled. 'Somebody let me out of here!'

The foam was spreading across the room, closer and closer towards Victoria, whose calls for help were being completely overwhelmed by the swelling sound of the creature's heartbeat . . .

'There it is, Jamie! Can you hear it?'

The Doctor was listening through his stethoscope, which was pressed up against the wall of the transparent pipeline tube. His face was tense and anxious.

Jamie could also hear the deadly sound, pulsating, thumping, pounding through the pipeline. He swallowed hard, and said, 'Aye. What is it?'

'It's the same sound I heard in the pipeline on the beach. I tell you, there's definitely something inside the . . . '

A penetrating scream suddenly echoed along the pipeline. There was no mistaking who it belonged to.

'*Doctor! Jamie!*' Victoria was screaming hysterically. '*Help me!*'

'That's Victoria!' said Jamie, staring inside the pipeline tube as if expecting to see Victoria trapped inside.

'*Help me!*'

The Doctor and Jamie wasted no more time. They left the pipeline tube, and rushed straight out of the room.

Victoria's frenzied calls for help were soon reverberating around the entire Refinery.

In the Control Hall, the commotion caused chaos amongst the crew. Everyone was trying to establish where the screams were coming from. Van Lutyens rushed off to the Impeller Area, leaving Robson to stare in confused disbelief at the pipeline tube running around the walls.

'*Doctor! Jamie! Help me!*'

Victoria's calls were becoming more and more desperate, more and more hysterical.

The Doctor and Jamie were rushing from one corridor to

another, but although Victoria's voice seemed to be getting closer and closer, they still couldn't find out how to get to her.

'Victoria!' yelled Jamie at the top of his voice.

'Victoria!' The Doctor's shouts were becoming frantic. 'Can you hear us, Victoria?'

A penetrating, prolonged scream.

The Doctor and Jamie stopped dead, and turned simultaneously.

Both of them were staring at the door of the Oxygen Store Room.

The thumping heartbeat sound was almost deafening. And, as thick white foam surged uncontrollably through the ventilator grille of the Oxygen Room, the tendrils of the Weed Creature weaved and quivered towards Victoria, closer and closer, hissing and popping . . .

Victoria screamed just one more time.

4

Mr Oak and Mr Quill

'Gas!' said the Doctor, listening to the hissing sound coming from beneath the door of the Oxygen Store Room.

Jamie was unable to answer. He was almost overcome by a violent fit of sneezing.

The Doctor tried to open the door. It was locked, with no sign of the key. 'Victoria!' he shouted, thumping on the door. 'Are you in there?'

Victoria's reply came almost immediately from the other side of the door. But her voice was now faint and barely audible. 'Doctor . . .'

'She's in there!' yelled the Doctor. 'Come on, Jamie!'

'Doctor . . . help me . . .'

'We're coming, Victoria! Hold on!'

The Doctor and Jamie folded arms, and stood back a pace or so. 'One . . . two . . . three!' With one enormous effort they lunged at the door, which burst open immediately.

Victoria was lying in a heap on the floor of the Oyxgen Room. Her eyes were half-open, and she could hardly breathe.

'Quick, Jamie!' said the Doctor, covering her mouth with his hand. 'Get hold of her!'

Jamie let out the most deafening sneeze, then helped the Doctor to lift Victoria and carry her out into the corridor.

'What's going on here?' Robson's rasping voice boomed out from the other end of the corridor. 'Who let you three out of the cabin?'

The Doctor and Jamie ignored him. They were too busy helping Victoria to revive.

Robson came hurrying down the corridor. Van Lutyens and the Chief Engineer were with him, but they went straight into the Oyxgen Store Room.

'Did you hear what I said?' Robson was yelling again. 'I gave strict orders that – '

'Mr Robson!' Van Lutyens, covering his mouth with his hand, was at the door of the Oxygen Room. 'In here. Gas!'

'Then find out what it is.'

Van Lutyens disappeared back into the Oxygen Room.

The colour was gradually returning to Victoria's pale cheeks. 'It was horrible!' she said to the Doctor, still struggling to breath clearly. 'That awful creature. What was it?'

The Doctor was immediately tense. 'Creature?'

'You . . . you didn't see it?' She turned around to look back into the Oxygen Room. 'In there?'

The Doctor, Jamie, and Robson looked into the room. It was now fully lit.

'It came . . . straight at me . . . an awful hissing sound . . . and foam . . . and it was covered in weed or something . . . oh, I don't know . . . ' Recounting her ordeal was clearly distressing Victoria. Her eyes were wide with fear. 'It came closer . . . and closer. Then I screamed, and . . . ' She covered her face with her hands, and dissolved into tears.

'It's all right, Victoria,' said the Doctor, holding her close in his arms protectively. 'You're quite safe now.'

Robson was glaring at Victoria cynically. 'Creatures indeed. The girl's hysterical!'

'Mr Robson!'

Robson turned to find the Chief Engineer standing in the doorway of the Oxygen Room.

'Some of the cylinders are empty! The seals are broken.'

Robson swung back angrily to Victoria. 'What have you been up to in there?'

Victoria wiped tears from her cheeks with the back of her hand, then replied quickly. 'I was hiding. I heard someone coming, and just went in.'

Robson was glaring at her. 'You broke in, didn't you?'

'No!'

'This door is always kept locked. You broke in and emptied those cylinders!'

'That's not true!' Victoria was regaining her defiant spirit. 'The door was open. Someone locked it behind me.'

Jamie stepped forward. He looked as though he was ready to strike Robson. 'She's telling the truth,' he said menacingly. 'The door was locked from the outside.'

'Mr Robson!'

The interruption of van Lutyens's voice was good excuse for Robson to ignore Jamie's threatening glare, and to go off into the Oxygen Room.

Van Lutyens and the Chief Engineer were removing their gas masks as Robson, the Doctor, Jamie, and Victoria entered the Oxygen Store Room. Everything seemed to be perfectly normal, and not at all as Victoria had described her encounter with the Weed Creature.

'Now what?' snapped Robson, impatiently.

Van Lutyens finished closing a tap on one of the oxygen cylinders, then turned to Robson with a grave, puzzled expression. 'This room wasn't full of oxygen when we arrived,' he said. 'It was another gas, one of a toxic composition if I'm not mistaken.'

'Toxic?' Robson looked at the Dutchman as though he had gone stark raving mad. 'Are you trying to tell me it was a poisonous gas?'

'Exactly, sir.'

Robson paused a moment, trying to take it all in. His eyes

43

flicked hurriedly around the room. 'Where did it come from?'

'From there possibly.' This time it was the Doctor who was speaking. He was inspecting `the open ventilator grille.

The others came across to join him.

'Did you open this ventilator?' Van Lutyens asked Victoria.

Victoria was firm in her reply. 'No! It opened itself!'

'The person who locked you in must've done it,' said Jamie, running his fingers over the wire mesh of the grille. 'But how?'

The Doctor and van Lutyens were investigating the ventilator control panel on the wall. Its position on the dial was indicating *OPEN*.

Maggie Harris was having difficulty in breathing. From the moment she had been stung by the clump of seaweed, her mind had become confused and disoriented. In fact, there was very little she could remember of what actually happened to her, even though it had been less than half an hour ago. To add to that, she had a hacking cough, a piercing headache, and a pain in her injured hand that felt as though she was supporting a heavy weight.

'What is it, love?' Frank Harris was sitting with his wife on the bed, deeply concerned by her condition.

'I don't know . . . I feel so drowsy . . . and my hand . . .' Maggie was aimlessly rubbing her injured hand without actually looking at it.

'Let me see.' Harris gently took her hand, and looked at it closely. He could see no visible signs of any kind of sting, not even a swelling. 'It looks all right. What happened?'

Maggie had a vacant look in her eyes. 'I . . . I don't remember.'

Harris was watching his wife carefully. He was alarmed by her uncharacteristic lack of energy. He said quietly, 'You said you were stung or something?'

'Stung?' Maggie had to think about it for a moment. Then, without shifting her eyes, she said, 'Yes. Yes, it must've been that. I . . . I found the file you asked for . . . ' She stopped, turned to look her husband straight in the eyes, and gradually eased herself up from the bed. Her mind was wandering strangely. 'I wasn't allowed to take it.'

Harris stood up, cupped his wife's face gently between his hands, and asked, 'Who wouldn't allow you?'

Maggie had that vacant look in her eyes again. 'I . . . I don't know . . . ' Then, with a sudden flash of unexpected anger, she pulled Harris's hands away from her and said, *It was the seaweed!*'

Harris was just in time to catch Maggie as she collapsed. 'All right love,' he said, trying not to panic. 'Just lie down and rest.' He lowered her back onto the bed, and made her comfortable. He smoothed her forehead with his hand, then kissed it gently. 'What you could do with is some food.'

Although Maggie's eyes were closed, she managed a more characteristic smile. 'Poor darling,' she said softly. 'You can't even boil an egg!'

Harris laughed. He was relieved that this was more like the Maggie he knew and loved. 'It serves you right for marrying a scientist . . . '

Maggie's recovery was short-lived. Her smile quickly faded, and with her eyes still closed, she slowly raised her head from the pillow. She seemed to be listening to something.

Harris, alarmed again, took hold of Maggie's shoulders. 'Darling? What is it?'

Maggie's face was absolutely rigid. Her mind was focussed elsewhere, drowned beneath a series of alien sounds which raced in and out of her subconscious like the endless roar of jetliners. The subliminal images she was receiving were coming from her own kitchen patio outside. She could 'see' the seaweed clump where she had thrown it, nestling in a bed of foam. And the bubbles and the weed popping, to emit a gaseous vapous. And the relentless hissing, thumping,

45

heartbeat sound, growing in intensity, tearing into Maggie's brain until she could bear it no more . . .

Maggie's eyes sprang open suddenly. She was staring straight into Harris's face. It looked distorted, like a gargoyle.

'What is it, love?' Harris was shaking her. 'Tell me!'

His voice seemed to boom out like thunder, and Maggie clutched her ears in pain.

'Are you ill, Maggie? Tell me!'

It took Maggie a moment or so to focus. When she did, her voice was barely audible. 'I . . . I don't know,' she whispered. 'I just feel . . . I don't know . . . '

Harris became immediately urgent. He lowered Maggie's head gently to the pillow, and said, 'I'm going back to see if Doc Patterson's returned from the rig yet.' He stood up, pulled the duvet over Maggie, and tucked her in. 'Will you be all right?'

Maggie didn't answer. She closed her eyes again, and just nodded her head.

Harris kissed her gently on the forehead, then went to the door. 'If Doc Patterson's not back, there's another Doctor that's turned up at the Refinery. He may be able to help.'

Again Maggie didn't answer. She seemed to be falling asleep.

Harris took one last anxious look at his wife, then left.

For a moment or so, Maggie remained still and silent. She was breathing heavily, but felt no real discomfort.

As the thaw continued outside, long icicles from the roof began to melt. Their intermittent dripping sounds onto the window-sill could almost have been notes from a song. A warning song perhaps.

Maggie was falling deeper and deeper into sleep. The song of the icicles could have been a million years away in comparison to the sounds that were again creeping into her subconscious. Thumping. Pulsating. The pounding of a heartbeat.

Maggie's eyes sprang open. But she was not awake. The thumping sound was closer, and she lay there listening to it. Then, almost as though on the word of a command, she threw off the duvet, rose up from the bed, and walked slowly towards the door. As she left the room, the last of the icicles outside finally melted.

Out into the hall, then into the kitchen. Maggie had no sense of where she was, or what she was doing. Her eyes were wide open, but she was fast asleep. She was living through a nightmare where some mystical force was commanding her to do something. But what?

As Maggie entered the kitchen, the heartbeat sounds were becoming louder and louder, faster and faster. The door! The door to the back patio! That's where Maggie was determined to go, *had* to go. But she didn't know why. Like an ethereal angel, she seemed to glide across the kitchen floor, step by perilous step, closer and closer towards her destiny. At last, she was at the door. Her hands blindly searched for the handle. They clasped it with a grip of iron. Slowly, it began to turn . . .

Maggie paused. Her own heartbeat was now competing with the one on the other side of that door. In one swift movement, she pulled open the door.

The noise was horrific. Thumping. Pulsating. Shrieking. Hissing. The seaweed clump was expanding in size, out of control.

Maggie clutched her ears in agony, slammed the door, and locked it. Rubbing her eyes, struggling to breathe, she just stood with her back to the door, totally bewildered. It was as though she had suddenly been awoken from a nightmare.

'What's all the panic?' Robson was pushing his way through a crowd of engineers who were anxiously watching a cluster of meters on the wall of the Impeller Area.

'It's the pump, sir!' said the Chief Engineer, urgently. The strain of the past few hours was beginning to catch up on him, for his eyes were glazed with tiredness. 'The revs have dropped.'

'The pump is slowing down, ja?' Van Lutyens was clearly shocked by this new development, for it was very rare that he slipped back into his native language, even one word of it.

The Chief Engineer tapped one of the meters with two of his fingers, then checked it for any change in movement. 'She's not holding steady even now,' he said nervously. 'I don't understand it!'

'Well, don't just stand there looking at it, man!' Robson was literally pushing the other engineers out of his way. 'Do a complete check!'

'Excuse me. D'you mind if I make a suggestion?'

Robson turned around with a glare to see the Doctor calling from the back of the group.

'When I was in your pipeline room just a short while ago, I distinctly heard some kind of movement coming from inside the pipeline tube. It was identical to the movement I heard coming from inside the pipeline on the beach,' said the Doctor in a stern voice. 'A thumping, pulsating type of sound.'

Van Lutyens immediately became very animated. 'That is what they heard out on the rigs!'

'Nonsense!' snarled Robson, aware that alarm was being generated amongst his crew. 'What they heard and what everyone's heard is a mechanical fault somewhere along the line!'

'But why did they hear it way out on the rigs?' insisted the Doctor.

'Because, my friend, beneath this impeller shaft is a vast steel gasometer buried in the earth. It's like an echo chamber. Drop even a pin down there and it'll sound like a thunderclap! Any sound down there travels along the pipeline.'

Robson's theory seemed logical, but unconvincing.

'But this sound wasn't mechanical,' retorted van Lutyens.

There was no doubt that Robson was now on the defensive. 'All right!' he thundered. 'Suppose it wasn't mechanical. Suppose there *is* something in the pipeline, a fish or something. What d'you expect me to do about it?'

The Doctor was first to reply. 'Turn off the gas flow until you've had a chance to check.'

'Out of the question!'

'But Mr Robson,' pleaded van Lutyens, 'if something *is* inside the – '

Robson was adamant. 'We do *not* turn off the flow. And that's final!'

'Down another half, sir!' The Chief Engineer was tapping the pressure meter again.

Robson pushed him aside to look at the meter himself. 'It *must* be a mechanical fault!' he snapped. 'Get a couple of men in here, and double-check!'

'Yes, sir!' The Chief Engineer rushed out.

Van Lutyens wiped the sweat from his forehead, and took an anxious look at the pressure meter. The indicator needle was flickering perilously close to the red danger level.

'If you allow the pressure to build up much more in that pipeline!' said the Dutchman, turning to Robson, 'you'll blow the Control Rig sky-high!'

'And all of us with it,' warned the Doctor.

Van Lutyens stared defiantly straight into Robson's eyes. 'Just because you're too stubborn to turn off the gas!'

There was a delayed reaction from Robson, which seemed like hours to the crew who were watching tensely.

'So what d'you think it is then?' There was a restrained but acid calm in Robson's eventual reply. 'Some more of these creature things that hysterical girl is supposed to have seen?'

'Who knows?' answered the Doctor. His face revealed just the hint of a wry smile.

In the Control Hall, Price was showing Jamie and Victoria the lay-out of the communications system.

'You mean, this place supplies gas to the whole of the south of England?' asked Jamie, casting his eyes over the maze of computer monitors on the huge Cone structure.

'Not only England,' replied Price. 'Wales too.'

Victoria's face was illuminated by a succession of different coloured lights, flashing on and off all over the Cone. 'What are all these lights for?' she asked, looking totally bewildered.

Price nodded towards a computerised board. 'That's a plan of the entire Refinery Compound. Each light represents a remote-controlled camera that I can switch through to my own personal monitor if I want to check with a particular area.'

Jamie scratched his head, trying hard to take in all the technical information. 'What about these rigs they keep talking about?'

'The rigs are out at sea,' said Price. He was now looking up at the huge illuminated panel on top of the Cone. 'That panel up there shows the relative position of all of them.'

'What's the big one . . . there in the middle?' asked Victoria. She was referring to a large red-coloured oblong shape in the centre of the panel.

'That's our main Control Complex Rig, the nerve centre of the entire group. The other rigs feed her with the gas, and she pumps it through to us via the main pipeline.'

'How horrible to have to live out there in the sea all that time,' said Victoria, bringing the conversation down to a more human level. 'And lonely.'

'Oh, I don't know,' said Price. 'Mr Robson spent nearly four years on one of the early rigs. He never came ashore once.'

'Aye,' said Jamie acidly. 'That accounts for quite a lot.'

Jamie had no sooner spoken when Robson himself came out of the Impeller Area. Van Lutyens and the Doctor were with him.

'Doctor! I need your help!'

The Doctor turned, to see Harris hurrying across the Hall from the compound entrance.

'It's my wife. She's very ill.'

'I'm sorry, Mr Harris,' said the Doctor awkwardly. 'You see I'm not really a - '

50

'Our own doctor is still out at Rig D. There's no one else I can turn to.' There was desperation in Harris's voice. 'You *must* come. Right away!'

'He's going nowhere!' interrupted Robson, firmly.

'But this is an emergency,' insisted Harris.

'These people are in my custody until I decide what to do with them.'

'But my wife . . . ' Harris was almost pleading.

Robson thumped his fist on the side of the Cone. 'Damn you, Harris! I won't have you bringing your domestic problems into this refinery.' Then he turned and shouted at the rest of his crew working in the Hall. 'And that goes for the lot of you!'

Harris was appalled. This time Robson had gone too far. 'Mr Robson,' he said through clenched teeth, 'my wife is ill. If anything happens to her, I'll . . . '

Robson was completely taken aback by his second-in-command's defiance. But he had been long enough in the business to know that if he lost the respect of his crew, there was nothing left. 'All right, Mr Harris,' he replied, without blinking his eyes. 'One hour!'

'Mrs Harris?'

'Yes?'

'We're maintenance controllers, madam. I wonder if we could have a few words with your husband?'

Maggie had answered her front door to two men. One of them was small and fat. The other was tall and thin. Both of them were dressed in white cap, tunic, and trousers. They looked like medical orderlies.

Maggie rubbed her eyes and tried to focus. She was absolutely drained of all energy. 'My husband isn't here,' she said. 'He's at the Compound.'

It was Mr Oak who replied. He was the small, fat one, with a cherubic, almost circular face, which seemed to be fixed in a perpetual smile. 'Oh dear,' he said, 'that does make it rather difficult. We have to carry out an inspection.'

51

'Inspection?'

'Your gas cooker, madam. In the kitchen.'

Maggie looked blank.

Mr Oak exchanged a puzzled look with his colleague. Then he turned back to Maggie and said, 'Your husband didn't tell you?'

'No, he didn't,' sighed Maggie wearily. 'Look, I'm not feeling very well. Can't it wait until another day?'

Mr Oak shook his head, but retained his smile. 'Oh, I'm afraid not, madam. It's got to be done without delay. Chief Robson's instructions.'

Maggie groaned. 'Chief Robson! That man never stops giving out instructions. Well, I suppose you'd better come in.' She opened the door wide, and stood back.

'Thank you, madam,' said Mr Oak, bowing politely. 'After you, Mr Quill.'

The tall, thin man entered the hallway first. He was carrying a small black leather bag. Mr Oak followed him in.

'Allow me to introduce ourselves, madam,' said small and fat. 'My name's Mr Oak. And this is my colleague, Mr Quill.'

Mr Quill didn't speak. In fact he never spoke. He slightly raised his cap, and bowed politely.

Maggie closed the front door and said impatiently, 'Could you please be quick? I really am not very well.' She pointed to a door on the other side of the hallway. 'That's the kitchen.'

'Thank you madam,' said Mr Oak. 'And don't you worry about us. You won't even know we're here. Will she, Mr Quill?'

Maggie disappeared quickly back into her bedroom. Only then did Mr Oak's smile finally fade. He nodded to tall and thin, and they both went into the kitchen.

Mr Quill went straight to the back patio door of the kitchen, and for a moment just stared at it. His pale, gaunt, funereal features were quite impassive.

'The bag, Mr Quill,' said short and fat. He was already

inspecting the cooker they were supposed to be servicing.

Mr Quill took the small black leather bag to the cooker, placed it on a working top alongside, and opened it.

Mr Oak reached into the bag, and took out two pairs of plain white gloves . . .

'Mr Robson, sir!' Price was calling from the Control Cone. 'Message from Control Rig!'

Robson was on the observation platform, checking temperature gauges. 'What do they want?' he yelled.

'There's an excessive pressure build-up in their pipeline feed to us!'

Robson hurried across to the Cone, snatched the tele-kation print-out message from Price. 'Ask them how much,' he ordered.

'Mr Robson!' Van Lutyens was rushing across from the Impeller Area. 'Pressure's almost up to danger level. Shall I give the order to turn off the flow?'

'You'll do nothing of the sort, Mr van Lutyens.'

'But the pressure is almost up to capacity,' warned van Lutyens, again mopping beads of sweat from his forehead. 'There will be an explosion at any minute!'

Robson flicked his eyes up from the message he was reading. 'There will *not* be an explosion,' he said, confidently.

The Dutchman stared at Robson in total disbelief, and said, 'If you don't turn off the flow, there's no way you can avoid it!'

Robson lost his patience, turned his back on the Dutch-man and yelled out to an engineer on the observation platform. 'Open Beach Release Valve, Section D. Full capacity!'

The engineer paused, unsure whether he had heard right.

Robson yelled again. 'Did you hear what I said?'

This time the engineer obeyed immediately, and started turning a valve wheel to release gas pressure in the specified section.

'What are you doing?' shouted van Lutyens. He was now convinced that Robson had completely misread the situation. 'You will never release enough gas in time!'

Robson's only reply was to turn with a sneering look at the Dutchman and say, 'D'you want to bet – *Mr* van Lutyens?'

The curtains were drawn in the Harrises' bedroom. Maggie was feeling much worse. Even though there was only a dim half-light in the room, she was lying flat on her back on the bed, covering her face with her hands, shielding her eyes from the light.

The silence was eventually broken by a gentle tapping sound, coming from the kitchen. The two maintenance controllers were clearly in the middle of their work on the gas cooker.

Maggie took her hands away from her face, and squinted. She again had a pounding headache. After lying there for a few minutes, she managed to summon up enough energy to pull herself up from the bed and cross the room. She sat down at the dressing table, and looked at her reflection in the mirror. The shock was immediate. Not only was she looking very tired and drawn, but, in her mind's eye, she was beginning to age prematurely.

In the kitchen, Mr Oak and Mr Quill were carrying out their mock inspection of the gas cooker. Not a word passed between them.

Almost by word of command, the two men suddenly stopped work. They could hear the approach of the thumping, heartbeat sound. Both men looked at each other. Mr Oak smiled. It was time for the real work to begin.

Mr Oak stretched out his hand to the cooker, and turned on each one of the taps. As he did so, he noticed the strands of seaweed that were beginning to form on his hand and arm. Both he and Mr Quill reacted to this with a triumphant glow in their eyes. Again, Mr Oak smiled. Then he picked up a pair of white gloves, similar to those which Mr Quill was already wearing, and put them on. Then both men turned to look at the back patio door.

The thumping, heartbeat sound was becoming louder, and more intense.

Mr Quill went to the back door, and opened it. The noise was immediately deafening. Thumping. Pulsating. Shrieking. Hissing. On the kitchen patio outside, the clump of seaweed had expanded into a solid mass, engulfed in a sea of bubbling white foam.

Mr Oak and Mr Quill left the room, and went out into the hallway. As they did so, bubbling white foam began seeping over the kitchen step through the open door.

Maggie was still sitting at her dressing table, resting her head wearily between her hands. On a sudden impulse, she determined to pull herself together. Grabbing her comb, she started tidying her hair. But as she looked up into the mirror, she gasped with a shocked start. The silhouettes of two figures were reflected there, standing behind her. Maggie swung round.

'What are you doing in here!' she yelled.

Mr Oak and Mr Quill did not reply. They remained absolutely still, just staring at Maggie.

Maggie looked terrified. She slowly rose, her back pressed against the mirror. 'You have no right to come into my room . . . ' Her hands were gripping hard the edge of the dresssing table.

Mr Oak and Mr Quill did not reply.

'Did you hear what I – '

Maggie did not finish her sentence. Her eyes suddenly flicked straight past the two intruders, to the open doorway. A wall of bubbling white foam and seaweed was pushing its way into the room. Maggie was too chilled with fear to speak. All she could do was to look on helplessly as the advance guard of the foam and weed began to snake its way across the room in her direction.

Mr Oak and Mr Quill took a few steps towards Maggie, then stopped within just a few feet of her. Both their faces were fixed with almost identical grins.

Maggie tried to scream. But she was stopped abruptly, as

Mr Oak and Mr Quill simultaneously took a deep breath, and opened their mouths as wide as they could. Then, in unison, they exhaled straight at Maggie. The sound they made was eerie and terrifying. It was the sound of hissing gas.

Maggie was immediately overcome by the fumes. She tried desperately to scream, but couldn't.

The bubbling white foam and weed was drawing closer and closer . . .

Maggie was clutching her throat, coughing, spluttering. She couldn't breathe.

Mr Oak and Mr Quill were immovable, like marble statues. The hissing sounds of gas fumes was still pouring out from their wide-open mouths.

Maggie was losing control, and could hold on no longer. As she slumped to the floor, she grabbed at the dressing table, scattering the contents all around her.

As the wall of foam and seaweed drew closer and closer to Maggie's lifeless body, the sound of hissing gas continued unabated from the wide-open mouths of Mr Oak and Mr Quill . . .

Somewhere along a lonely stretch of beach, the hissing sound of gas continued. This time however, it was being released from the valve on top of the giant pipeline tube.

The hissing sound suddenly stopped. The valve was closed.

5

Waiting in the Dark

'It's down!' The Chief Engineer raised his fist triumphantly, after checking the pressure gauge on the wall of the Impeller Area. The needle was wavering to and fro frantically. 'The pressure in the pipeline – it's back to normal!'

A great cheer went up from the group of engineers who were watching anxiously.

'Congratulations, Mr Robson,' said van Lutyens with relief. 'I would not have thought you could have done it.'

Robson was glowing with self-confidence after the success of his decision to open the valve and release gas from the beach section of the pipeline. 'If you have too much gas in the tube, get rid of it!' he scowled bombastically. 'Didn't they ever teach you that in Training School back at the Hague, Mr van Lutyens?'

The Dutchman refused to answer. He had become immune to Robson's petty insults. Robson grinned, then turned to one of the engineers. 'Inform Baxter at Control Rig that the immediate crisis is over. And contact the other rig chiefs.'

The engineer rushed off to pass on the messages. Robson

and van Lutyens followed him out to the Control Hall, stopping at the observation platform to check various pressure gauges.

'What about the feed-out to the receiving stations?' asked the Dutchman. 'It's still dropping.' Robson ignored him and started tapping one of the gauges. The Dutchman persisted. 'The impeller is still slowing down . . .'

Robson suddenly lost his cool again. 'What's the matter with you, van Lutyens?' he growled. 'You've been trying to teach me my job ever since you came here. I've been drilling for gas out there in the North Sea most of my life. I don't need people like you, or Harris, to teach me how to do it!'

'Mr Robson!' Price was calling urgently from the Control Cone. There was a touch of hysteria in Price's voice. 'It's Rig C, sir. We can't raise them!'

Robson hurried across to the Cone, followed by van Lutyens.

'What d'you mean you can't raise them?' snapped Robson, as he looked at the video monitor screen used for contact with Rig C. It was streaked with distorted, quivering lines.

'We've tried everything, sir. There's no response at all!'

Robson ignored Price and started punching out video and computer keys. The monitor screen remained defiantly blank.

'So the immediate crisis is over, is it?' said the Dutchman to Robson ironically. He was also watching the blank monitor screen.

Frank Harris arrived home to find the front door of his apartment block wide open. 'Maggie!' he called out anxiously. 'I've brought the Doctor!'

The Doctor, Jamie, and Victoria followed Harris into the hallway. The moment they entered, Jamie became convulsed with a loud fit of sneezing.

'Gas!' yelled the Doctor. He and the others quickly covered their mouths.

Harris rushed into the bedroom and immediately shouted

58

back to the Doctor to follow him. The Doctor, Jamie, and Victoria charged into the bedroom, and were nearly choked by the smell of gas fumes.

'Maggie!' Harris went straight to his wife, who was slumped in a heap on the floor. Everyone was coughing and spluttering.

'Quick, Jamie!' the Doctor shouted. 'The window!'

Jamie desperately searched around for something to break open the window. His eyes lighted on a heavy wooden chair, and, in a split-second decision, he smashed the window open with it, splintering glass everywhere.

The deadly gas fumes were instantly sucked out of the room, to be replaced by a stream of ice-cold air from outside. The Doctor, Jamie, and Victoria stayed by the broken window, taking deep breaths of fresh air.

Frank Harris, distraught and desperate, was kneeling beside the lifeless body of his wife. Maggie's eyes were firmly closed, and her face was as white as sea foam. 'Maggie . . . ' called Harris, gently caressing her face with his hand. 'Oh, Maggie . . . '

In the Control Hall at the Refinery, the video monitor screen was still flickering with distorted lines.

'I'm sorry, sir,' said Price nervously. 'We've completely lost contact with Rig C.'

Robson clenched his fist and punched it into his other hand in frustration. Then he turned away from the Cone, deep in thought. Van Lutyens pursued him.

'I hope you are satisfied with what you've done?' The Dutchman's booming voice echoed around the Hall, causing everyone to stop what they were doing.

Robson turned slowly. With seething rage he was glaring at the Dutchman. 'Van Lutyens,' he sneered. 'I'm warning you . . . '

'And I warned you!' roared van Lutyens defiantly. 'But you were too stubborn to listen. Look at the facts, man, the facts!'

Robson strode off. Again the Dutchman pursued him. 'First we lose contact with two rigs,' continued van Lutyens. 'Then, for over three weeks we have unprecedented and inexplicable pressure variations in the entire pipeline system.'

'Oh, so that's it!' yelled Robson, stopping dead on the steps of the observation platform. 'You've been talking with Harris!'

'Only because you refuse to listen to his calculations!' The Dutchman was matching Robson's outburst with his own anger. 'That's why I went out to the Control Rig – to see if there was any explanation out there!'

'And what did you find?' Robson snapped back. His exchange with van Lutyens had now become a shouting match. 'Nothing! And I'll tell you why – because there was nothing to find!'

'I tell you Mr Harris's figures are – '

'To hell with Harris and his figures!' Robson's face was now blood-red with fury, and a vein protruded from his forehead. 'D'you think I'm going to take notice of some schoolkid, with his bits of paper, graphs and sliderule? I've spent my life on this job. I know every nut and bolt on every rig out in that sea!'

Van Lutyens sighed despondently. He had long been aware of Robson's antipathy towards Harris's red-brick university education. 'All right,' said the Dutchman, 'so your prejudice prevents you from accepting Mr Harris's calculations. But what about me? Do you dismiss my opinion with as much contempt?'

'You?' Robson's glare turned into a cynical smile. 'You, Mr van Lutyens, are here to offer your expert advice. However, I am not obliged to take it. This is my outfit, and I run it the way I want to. Understood?'

'Mr Robson!' Robson swung with a start, to see an engineer calling from the door of the Impeller Area.

'The impeller! She's down to 140 revs. Something must be jamming her at the base.'

Robson rushed into the impeller area. Van Lutyens followed him. The Chief Engineer was frantically tapping pressure gauges, stopping only to listen to the impeller Housing Unit. His crew were anxiously staring down into the darkness of the impeller shaft, where the sound of the giant pump was gradually slowing down.

Everyone was watching and waiting tensely. The giant pump was moving erratically now, crunching and grating with enormous effort. Finally, it ground to a halt with a huge thud.

The silence that followed seemed unnatural. No one could remember a time when the sound of the giant impeller pump had not dominated the life of the Refinery.

'All right, Mr Robson,' called van Lutyens, breaking the silence. 'Where do we go from here?'

Robson was staring in disbelief at the giant pump. He refused to reply or even look at the Dutchman.

Van Lutyens persisted. 'Well, come on! You have all the answers, don't you?'

'Quiet! Everyone!'

The Chief Engineer had his ear pressed up against the perspex case of the Impeller Housing Unit. Robson and the others joined him.

'What is it?' asked the Dutchman in a hushed voice.

The Chief Engineer closed his eyes whilst he tried to listen. Without turning, he said, 'I think I can hear something . . . '

Frank Harris's face was ashen-white with distress as he held the lifeless body of his wife in his arms.

Victoria and Jamie were anxiously watching the Doctor examine Maggie with his stethoscope. Victoria swallowed hard, then plucked up courage to ask timidly, 'Is she – dead?'

The Doctor removed his stethoscope. 'No, she's not,' he replied.

Everyone breathed a sigh of relief, especially Harris. 'Then what's the matter with her?' he asked.

'She's in some sort of coma,' said the Doctor sternly. 'Possibly because of that gas.' He removed the stethoscope from his ears, then looked Harris straight in the face. 'It was toxic.'

Harris was shocked. 'That's impossible,' he said. 'Natural gas isn't toxic.'

'This wasn't natural gas. It's the same sort of gas we found when Victoria was locked in the Oxygen Room.'

Harris was even more puzzled. 'But where could it have come from?'

'That's what I'd like to know,' muttered the Doctor, taking a quick, suspicious look around the room. Then he resumed his examination of Maggie, pulling open one of her eyelids to see if there was any sign of movement in the lifeless, staring pupil. 'What exactly did she say happened to her?' he asked.

'Something about being stung by a clump of seaweed.'

To anyone else, Harris's reply would have sounded absurd, bizarre. But not to the Doctor, Jamie, or Victoria, who all reacted with a simultaneous look at Harris.

'Seaweed!' said Jamie, turning suddenly from the smashed window.

'I asked Maggie to get a file from my study. Apparently she found the seaweed on top of it.'

'A curious place to find such a thing,' remarked the Doctor carefully. 'Did you put the seaweed there, Mr Harris?'

Harris took exception to this. 'No! Certainly not!'

The Doctor did not pursue the point. He decided instead to resume his examination of Maggie. 'There don't appear to be any marks or abrasions.'

'Doctor!'

Everyone turned to look at Victoria, who was cowering from something on the floor nearby. It was a small clump of seaweed.

'Seaweed!' said Jamie, stooping down to take a close look at the clump. 'What's it doing here?'

Harris gently lowered his wife back onto the bed, then joined the others, who were all cautiously watching the seaweed clump.

'It's still quite wet,' observed the Doctor, studying the clump from all angles.

'Perhaps this is what Maggie was talking about,' said Harris, stooping down to pick up the intruder.

'No! Don't touch it!' yelled the Doctor, grabbing Harris by the shoulder and yanking him back.

'Why?' said the astonished Harris.

'Your wife said she was stung by a clump of seaweed, remember?'

Harris swung a look of incredulity at the clump.

'Furthermore,' continued the Doctor. 'I have a feeling that whoever put that seaweed on top of your file meant *you* to touch it.'

'Me?' Harris brushed his usual lock of hair from his eye. 'Wait a minute,' he said, suddenly remembering something. 'I was sure I put that file in my briefcase this morning, but it wasn't there when I went to get it. I was on my way home to collect the file, but I met Maggie and . . . ' He stopped, turned to look at the clump. 'But why? Why should anyone want me to get stung by a piece of seaweed?'

'I hate the stuff. It's so slimy and horrid.' Victoria stood well back from the clump. She was still chilled by the memory of her encounter with the Seaweed Creature.

'Och,' said Jamie, teasing Victoria, 'you've seen plenty of seaweed before. The beach near the pipeline was crawling with the stuff this morning.'

'Yes,' replied Victoria, her gaze transfixed on the wet, slimy clump on the floor. 'And that moved too. Just like this one.'

Jamie's eyes widened with horror. '*Moved?*'

Everyone was now staring at Victoria.

No-one was standing around idly in the Impeller Area. The place was buzzing with activity, with engineers rushing in and out, checking and adjusting every control valve in sight.

'I want them all checked!' The Chief Engineer was yelling out orders to all the men around him. 'Every remote-controlled release valve on the line. Check and double-check the circuits!' Crewmen bustled to their individual jobs, one of them colliding with van Lutyens as he hurried into the area.

'Chief!' called the Dutchman, who was carrying a rolled-up technical diagram under his arm. 'This impeller is still not working?'

'Not yet, sir!'

'What about the noise you heard in the pipeline? Have you heard it again?'

'No, I haven't sir,' replied the Chief, then added unconvincingly, 'Mr Robson was probably right. It's just a mechanical fault somewhere.'

The Dutchman cringed. He just refused to believe that someone as skilled as the Chief Engineer would accept such a basic theory. 'And you believe that?' he said.

The Chief Engineer avoided van Lutyen's glance, then answered awkwardly, 'It's not really my job to question someone in authority, sir.'

Van Lutyens sighed despondently. 'Chief, could you come outside for a moment? I'd like a word with you in private.'

The Chief hesitated, nodded, then followed van Lutyens out into the Control Hall.

'I've been studying the layout of the installation,' said the Dutchman quietly, 'and in particular, the impeller intake. I think I know where the blockage may be.' He found the nearest available table, and spread out the technical diagram he was carrying. It showed the complete layout of the impeller intake system. 'Look here,' he continued, indicating a specific set of valves on the diagram. 'This valve at the base of the main shaft: it leads directly into the intake. Is that correct?'

The Chief Engineer studied the diagram briefly, then nodded. 'Yes, sir.'

'Now as far as I can see, there's no other point between that valve and the Control Rig which could cause a blockage sufficient to stop the impeller.'

'Apart from the undersea emergency valves, sir.'

Van Lutyens took a quick look at the Chief. 'But you have remote-control observation of those, and they're free – yes?'

'Yes.'

Van Lutyens took a red pen from out of his pocket. 'Then the main impeller valve is obviously the fault?' On the diagram he drew a red circle around the offending valve.

'It's possible, sir,' replied the Chief without committing himself.

'Possible!' Van Lutyens was losing his patience with the Chief. 'Look, man, it's the only answer. What we've got to do is get down there and clear that valve.'

The Chief Engineer hesitated. 'I'd have to check with Mr Robson to do that, sir.'

'Robson! Robson!' exploded the Dutchman, quickly rolling up the diagram again. 'What are you all, children or something that you can't do anything on your own initiative?'

'I'm sorry, sir. I can't send men down that shaft without Mr Robson's approval.' The Chief turned his back on the Dutchman, and hurried off towards the impeller area. Van Lutyens followed him.

'And can you not also blow your own nose without approval?' yelled the Dutchman.

The Chief Engineer replied from the door of the impeller area, but he did not raise his voice. 'Now, listen to me, Mr van Lutyens. I've worked with Mr Robson a long time. We were out on the rigs together in the early days. Now, you may think he's wrong to run the place the way he does – that's your privilege. But I trust him. I take orders from him simply because I respect his judgement, and for no other reason.'

Van Lutyens had to respect the Chief Engineer for the honest way he had spoken, and felt slightly ashamed of his own outburst. After the Chief had returned to the impeller area, van Lutyens hesitated for a moment, then followed him.

'All right Chief,' said the Dutchman, in a calm, more compromising approach. 'At least go to Robson and tell him where we think the blockage is. Get his official permission to inspect the base of shaft.'

The Chief was quick to reply. 'With respect, sir, that's your theory, not mine.'

'But it's the *only* possibility!' Van Lutyens suddenly realised that without the sound of the giant impeller, his voice could be heard by everyone around him. He quickly drew closer to the Chief, and spoke quietly. 'Look. Those voices you heard. They couldn't have come from anywhere but the base of the shaft.'

The Chief was finding it hard to come up with a rational explanation. 'If the main valve was open, they could have been echoes from any one of the rigs.'

'Yes, *if* it is open,' said the Dutchman fervently. He was practically whispering straight into the Chief's ear. 'But you don't know, and you won't know until you check!'

There was a pause. For once, the Chief had no answer. He turned around to see all his crewmen looking at him, as though waiting for him to make some kind of positive decision. 'Well,' he finally spoke, rubbing his chin anxiously, 'I suppose I could put it to Mr Robson . . . '

Van Lutyens sighed with relief and hope.

'But I'm warning you, he's not going to take kindly to . . . '

'Listen!' Van Lutyen's voice silenced the Chief immediately. Everyone stopped what they were doing.

They could hear a sound. It was only a faint, distant sound. But it was certainly there, gradually gaining in volume. Thumping. Like a heartbeat.

Everyone automatically looked up at the pipeline tube.

66

The thumping sound was echoing inside, as though some-thing was trapped there, trying to get out.

Van Lutyens and the Chief Engineer went straight to the edge of the impeller shaft, and looked down. The sound they could hear was clear, sharp, and threatening. 'Don't tell me that's a mechanical fault!' said the Dutchman in a tense, strangulated whisper.

'Chief!' Robson's voice boomed out from the open doorway. 'What the hell's going on here?'

The Chief turned with a start. 'That noise in the impeller, sir. It's started again. I think we should go down and check the main valve.'

'Oh, you do, do you?' Robson walked slowly towards the Chief, then stopped just in front of him. 'Why?'

'That's where we think the blockage is, sir.'

Although Robson was glaring at the Chief, it was really directed at the Dutchman. 'We?'

Van Lutyens stepped forward defiantly. 'Robson, there's something alive down there in that pipeline!'

'Alive?' Robson pushed the two men aside, looked down the impeller shaft, and listened.

There was absolute silence. No thumping. No heartbeat.

Robson turned to the Dutchman, and looked at him as though he was mad. 'You're out of your mind. There's nothing down there!'

The Chief quickly interceded. 'I promise you, sir, I *did* hear something . . . '

Robson ignored the Chief, and directed his fury towards the Dutchman. 'Van Lutyens, I'm warning you! You're stirring up my men, and they're behaving like a bunch of hysterical schoolgirls! Now get out of here!'

'Listen!' Van Lutyens was staring up at the pipeline tube.

'There it is again!' said the Chief, almost too afraid to hear the sound of his own voice.

Robson was ready to explode with anger at both men. 'Did you hear what I - '

'Shut up!' yelled the Dutchman, swinging around suddenly on Robson. 'Now, *listen!*'

Everyone gathered around the edge of the impeller shaft. As they listened, the thumping sound returned. Soon the pipeline tube was reverberating with the alien sound. Thumping. Pulsating. Bubbling. Closer and closer. Louder and louder.

There was shock and fear on the faces of everyone who was peering down the huge shaft.

'It's down there,' said the Dutchman, his voice barely a whisper. 'In that pipeline . . . in the darkness . . . waiting . . .'

The massive heartbeat was pumping furiously.

6

The Specimen

'No, Jamie! Don't touch it!' The Doctor was determined not to take any chances with the clump of seaweed, which was still nestling on the floor of Harris's bedroom.

'Och, why not?' said Jamie, his hand poised above the clump. 'It's only an odd bit of seaweed.'

'Maybe so. But if it did move, like Victoria said . . .'

Jamie withdrew his hand, and straightened up. 'How can a bit of seaweed move? It's not a living thing – is it?'

The Doctor twitched his eyebrows. 'Everything in the sea is living, Jamie.'

'I'm quite sure it moved,' insisted Victoria. After all she had been through with the seaweed creature, she was keeping well clear of the alien clump. 'It gave me a terrible fright. It was like a giant spider.'

'Well, we'd better not take any chances,' said the Doctor. Whilst he was talking, he took out of his inside jacket pocket a small polythene bag. 'Here, Jamie.' He shook out the bag, and gave it to Jamie. 'Hold this for me will you, please?'

Jamie was puzzled, but took the bag and held it open. 'What's it for?'

The Doctor stooped down to the seaweed clump. 'I think we'll take a closer look at this.' From another pocket, he took out a pencil, which he used to pick up the clump. 'Hold the bag down here, Jamie. Mind your fingers!'

Jamie held the rim of the bag wide open, and the Doctor carefully dropped the clump into it. 'What are you going to do with it, Doctor?' he asked.

The Doctor took the bag from Jamie. 'I'm going to find out if an ordinary piece of seaweed really can move.' He tied a knot in the bag, then held it up to take a closer look. The seaweed specimen did look a bit as Victoria had described it: like a huge spider curled up in a heap.

'Doctor.' Frank Harris was sitting on the bed trying to revive Maggie, who was still lying unconscious there. He looked in abject despair. 'My wife – will she be all right?'

The Doctor frowned before replying. 'I think so, Mr Harris. It's difficult to say. There's no immediate panic as far as I can see, but you'd better get her under medical supervision.'

'Yes,' said Harris. He got up from the bed, kissed Maggie gently on the forehead, looked at her anxiously, then joined the Doctor. 'I'll go back to the Medicare Centre at the Compound and arrange for her to be taken in there.'

The Doctor smiled reassuringly. 'Good idea.'

Harris went to the door, stopped to take one last worried look at his wife, then left.

'Poor man,' said Victoria, shaking her head with a sigh.

'Aye,' Jamie agreed, 'Hey! I thought we were supposed to be prisoners?'

The Doctor's eyes suddenly glistened with hope. 'So did I, Jamie!' he chuckled. 'We'd better make the most of it. We've got work to do back at the TARDIS.'

'What about Mrs Harris?' said Victoria.

The Doctor hurried across to the bed to take one quick last look at Maggie. 'She seems to be sleeping peacefully. Come on, let's get out of here!' He thrust the plastic bag into Jamie's hands, and rushed out. Jamie looked disgustedly at the seaweed specimen inside the polythene bag, pulled a face at it, then followed the Doctor. Last to leave was Victoria, who went to cover Maggie properly with the duvet. After a last anxious look, Victoria hurried off to join the others, quietly closing the door behind her.

Outside, the early afternoon light was becoming thinner. The thaw was still continuing, but there were signs of an approaching breeze, which caused the bedroom curtains at the smashed window to flutter restlessly.

Maggie was breathing quite normally, her eyes firmly closed. She seemed at peace. Suddenly, a movement: her hand slipped from beneath the duvet cover, and dangled to and fro aimlessly.

A frond-like weed formation was beginning to grow down Maggie's exposed hand and arm.

There was shock and fear on the group of faces peering down into the darkness of the impeller shaft. The giant pump itself was still immobile, but the thumping heartbeat sound continued to echo throughout the aluminium pipeline tube.

'In God's name, what *is* that sound?' The Chief Engineer was gripping the safety rail around the surface of the shaft, his voice reduced to a faltering whisper.

Van Lutyens, like the rest of the engineers, was almost mesmerised by the throbbing, pulsating sound coming up from the base of the shaft. 'It's uncanny,' he murmured. 'Like a . . . a heartbeat . . .'

Robson was clearly affected by the sound. Both his hands were gripping the safety rail, and his eyes were transfixed down into the darkness of the Shaft, as though he alone knew exactly what was going on down there.

And then, the unexpected happened. The thumping sound came to a sudden, dramatic halt.

The silence was deafening.

The Chief Engineer was first to speak. 'It's stopped again.' The rest of the crew were looking nervously around, down to the shaft, up to the pipeline tube.

71

Van Lutyens turned immediately to Robson. 'This surely must be proof.'

Robson had not relaxed his grip on the safety rail. He was still staring down into the shaft. 'Proof?' he murmured, as i in a trance. Suddenly, he swung around to look the Dutch man straight in the eyes. He hesitated, then burst into scornful laughter.

Van Lutyens watched Robson as though he was mad. He had to raise his voice to be heard. 'Proof that there i something down there blocking the impeller.'

'Rubbish!' snarled Robson, waving his hand dismissively 'Hysterical nonsense!'

'But you heard it. That terrible sound . . . '

Robson was unyielding. 'I heard a mechanical fault in the base of the impeller!'

Van Lutyens pointed in frustration towards the shaft. 'Bu the impeller isn't working! Don't you ever believe anything until you can see it?'

Robson had had enough. He pushed past the Dutchman and made for the door, yelling to the engineers as he went, ' want this impeller operational in half an hour!' He stopped at the door and turned. 'Now get to it!'

Through the transparent door, van Lutyens could see Robson disappearing back amongst the maze of electronic hardware in the Control Hall. The Dutchman was now more convinced than ever that the Refinery was being run by a lunatic.

Back inside the TARDIS, the Doctor dropped his seaweed specimen into a small glass tank. Attached to the side of the tank were two miniature metal cylinders containing two transparent tubes inserted through holes on either side of the tank.

Jamie peered at the specimen inside the tank and scratched his head in puzzlement. 'What are you doing, Doctor?'

Before replying, the Doctor covered the tank with its seal

tight lid. 'These cylinders contain a small quantity of natural gas, Jamie. It might be interesting to see what effect it has on the weed specimen – if any.' He turned on the cylinder release taps, and immediately the sound of hissing gas could be heard coming from inside the tank.

This corner of the TARDIS was beginning to look like a medical laboratory, for the Doctor had produced all sorts of bottles of chemical liquids and powders. There were also several large, dusty reference books piled up on the control console.

Victoria was at a workbench nearby, hearing some liquid in a test tube over a Bunsen flame. The bench was stacked with bottles and odd-shaped glass containers. 'How are you getting on, Victoria?' The Doctor came across to join her.

'I don't know,' replied Victoria, looking puzzled into the test tube. 'You'd better take a look.'

The Doctor took the tube from Victoria and held it up to the light. 'Nothing unusual. The seaweed contains the normal iron content.'

Victoria was still uneasy. 'Yes. But I did this other test, like you told me, and I found something which worries me.' She reached across to a bulb-shaped glass container, inside which was a small particle of the seaweed specimen floating in a colourless liquid. The sides of the container were tarnished with something which resembled rust, only just visible through a cloud vapour.

The Doctor looked into the container with great interest. 'I'm not surprised, Victoria,' he said, pointing to the brown stain around the bulb. 'Do you see the deposit? This means the weed contains some kind of gas – probably toxic.'

'Toxic?' Victoria exchanged a worried glance with the Doctor.

'Hey, Doctor!' Jamie was at the Doctor's table, peering into the microscope. 'What are these funny little bits moving about in the weed?'

The Doctor was still preoccupied with the contents of the glass bulb. 'Just a minute, Jamie. Don't worry me.' But he

73

suddenly turned with a start. 'What did you say?' He quickly put down the glass bulb, and rushed across to take over the microscope from Jamie.

'Can you see them?' said Jamie, peering over the Doctor's shoulder.

'Jamie! This is it!' The Doctor thumped the table jubilantly. 'There's molecular movement!'

'There's what?'

In great excitement, the Doctor pushed Jamie out of the way, rushed across to the control console, and pushed a button. The lights immediately faded into near darkness, and a flap on the wall revealed a large projector screen. Rubbing his hands with glee, the Doctor pressed another button. The microscope slide automatically appeared in magnified form on the screen. It showed a substance full of dots and squiggles, but with definite signs of molecular movement. The Doctor stared at the screen in wonder and bewilderment. 'Incredible! Absolutely incredible!'

'What is it, Doctor?' said Jamie, turning his head from side to side, trying to make some sense of the screen image. 'What does it mean?'

Victoria was also staring in amazement at the screen from her bench on the other side of the room. 'It means, Jamie, that the weed specimen is as much alive as you and me.'

Jamie swung a look of total disbelief at Victoria. Then he turned to the Doctor, who was nodding his head reluctantly.

None of them were yet aware of what was going on in the glass tank at the side of Victoria. The heartbeat sound was muffled within the sealed container.

The seaweed specimen was beginning to pulsate . . .

'Mr Harris, it's imperative we do something about Robson without delay. He just won't listen to reason.' Van Lutyens was in the Control Hall corridor, where he had been waiting to intercept Harris on his way back from the Compound.

'I'm sorry, van Lutyens,' replied Harris, whose nerves were now raw with anxiety, 'I've got something more important on my mind at the moment.' He tried to move on, but the Dutchman blocked his way.

'More important!' protested van Lutyens. 'What is more important than . . .'

'My wife is ill! Get out of the way!' Harris practically pushed the Dutchman aside, and rushed off into the Control Hall. Van Lutyens stared after him, bewildered, then followed.

'Price!'

'Sir!'

Harris was calling from the Compound exit door in the Control Hall. 'Doc Patterson still not back?'

'No, sir. We've heard nothing at all from Rig D.'

'Right. Get on to Matron at the Medicare Unit. Tell her to send a couple of orderlies over to my quarters with a stretcher to bring my wife in. She's been taken ill.'

'Right away, sir!' Price was already punching out computer keys to make contact with the Medicare Unit.

'Harris!' It was the unmistakeable voice of Robson, booming out from the office area. 'What's the panic now?'

Harris hurried across to him. 'It's my wife. She's been taken ill. She needs medical attention.'

Robson sighed irritably. 'What's the matter with her this time? Another headache?'

It took all of Harris's self-control to resist rising to Robson's jibes. 'She's very ill, Mr Robson,' he replied calmly.

'Oh yes?' persisted Robson with a sneer. 'And who says so? I suppose it was that Doctor bloke you . . . Wait a minute, where is he?' He flicked a quick glance around the Control Hall. 'And those two kids?'

Only at that moment did Harris realise what he'd done. His answer came out as a defensive stammer. 'I . . . I left them in my quarters when I . . .'

Robson's eyes were blazing with anger. 'You *what*?' He moved quickly towards Harris, almost as though he was going to hit him. 'They're supposed to be under guard, and you left them . . . in your own married quarters?'

'I was worried about my wife. I didn't have time to think about . . .'

'Those three prisoners were in your charge!'

'I don't care!' snapped Harris. 'Don't you understand? My wife was lying there on the floor when I got there. She was unconscious, and the place was stifled by the smell of toxic gas.' He brushed the lock of hair from his eye, then with every muscle in his face taut with tension, said, 'She's been poisoned, Robson! My wife's been poisoned!'

Van Lutyens was listening to Harris's outburst with rivetted interest. 'Mr Harris, you said your quarters were filled with toxic gas fumes?'

'Yes.'

'Where did they come from?'

'I have no idea.'

'No,' snapped Robson. 'And we shall none of us know now you've let those three go loose.' He turned his back on Harris and strode off. Harris followed him and said, 'How could they possibly have had anything to do with it?'

'It still doesn't alter the fact that you disobeyed my orders!' Robson stopped dead, and swung round on Harris again. 'You released those three prisoners without my authority.'

Harris was at the point of despair. 'Prisoners? A harmless old man and a couple of teenagers?'

Robson took a deep breath, and crossed his arms obstinately. 'That harmless old man, you're so fond of, is probably a saboteur! How d'you know he's not the one who's been tampering with that valve on the shoreline? Can't you get it into that thick head of yours that this Doctor bloke is responsible for producing those variations in pressure that you were getting so excited about!'

'Don't be so ridiculous, Robson!' Harris was now yelling at the Controller. 'You're clutching at straws, stupidly blind to the real facts!'

'Don't you shout at me, boy!' Robson yelled back.

A full-scale row was only averted by the Chief Engineer, who was calling from the open window of the impeller area.

'Mr Robson! The impeller!'

As he spoke, a slow grinding sound was heard. Everyone turned automatically to look towards the giant impeller.

'It's moving again!' called the Chief, triumphantly.

Robson threw a smug, cynical grin at Harris, then rushed into the impeller area. The others followed him.

Once again the impeller area was buzzing with activity. The Chief Engineer was labouring at the controls of the giant impeller, which was thumping up and down again, but with some difficulty. 'It just started up again, quite suddenly,' said the Chief, whose face was moist with sweat.

'All right, man, keep it moving!' snapped Robson, tensely watching the impeller's struggle to burst into action. But its movement was erratic, and there were already signs that it could not possibly sustain its recovery. Robson yelled again. 'Don't let it go now!'

Quite suddenly, the giant impeller once again came to a dramatic halt.

Robson was beside himself with rage. He stared in total disbelief at the impeller, refusing to accept that it would not budge. 'You fools!' he yelled to everyone in sight. 'You stupid fools!'

Everyone was amazed by Robson's wild outburst. He was glaring from one to the other of them as though they had all contrived to sabotage the impeller.

The Chief Engineer came to his men's defence. 'There was nothing we could do. It's jammed at the base.'

Robson could not be placated. He immediately turned on van Lutyens and Harris. 'You wanted this, didn't you?' He was ranting like a madman. 'It's just what you wanted!'

Van Lutyens retorted, 'You should have listened to me, Robson. You should have . . . '

'I should have what? Turned off the flow? Spoiled a reputation of thirty years!'

'Reputation!' Van Lutyens could hardly believe the illogic

of Robson's mind. 'Don't you realise that what's going on here is something totally outside your comprehension? That whatever it is that's in the pipeline, that's blocking the pump, that's taken over your rigs, is a threat, a menace to us all?'

Robson blinked his eyes at the Dutchman, but it was more of a twitch. 'Menace? Threat?' He burst into cynical laughter, even though it was quite obvious he was disturbed by what had happened, and was refusing to admit it. 'The only menace round here is you, van Lutyens. You and your friend Mr Harris there.'

The Dutchman and Harris exchanged a look of deep concern as Robson then rounded on the engineers. 'Well? What are you lot staring at?' he growled. 'I want this impeller in working order. Now get to it!' Finally, he turned back to Harris. 'I want to know immediately this impeller is in working order again. Understood – Mr Harris?' He hesitated for a moment, clutching his forehead as though he had a headache. Everyone was watching him, convinced that the Controller was beginning to break up under the strain of circumstances which he neither accepted or understood. With a final defiant glare at Harris and van Lutyens, Robson rushed back to the Control Hall.

Harris and van Lutyens exchanged a look of deep consternation. 'He's cracking up,' said the Dutchman. 'I think you'll have to take over soon.'

Harris shook his head. 'No, I've got to get back to my wife.' He turned to go, but van Lutyens caught him by the arm. 'Harris, you can't leave now,' the Dutchman pleaded. 'Can't you see Robson is losing control?'

Harris rubbed his eyes, which were sore with tension. 'My wife needs help . . . '

'Your wife will be brought back here to the Medicare Unit. She'll be kept under close supervision.'

'Damnit, van Lutyens!' snapped Harris. 'I have a duty towards my wife . . . '

'You also have a duty towards this refinery.' There was a

note of desperation in the Dutchman's voice. 'Listen, Harris. If Robson does crack up, as I think he's going to, then you are the only one with the authority to take over. We need you here.'

Harris was totally confused. He hesitated for a moment, then turned to the Chief Engineer, who had abandoned his struggle to re-activate the impeller pump. 'What do you think, Chief? You know Mr Robson better than any of us. How . . . I mean, d'you think he's fully aware of the situation?'

The Chief lowered his eyes uneasily. He had always tried his best to show loyalty towards the Controller, often under extreme provocation. 'Well, sir . . . Mr Robson's under a great deal of strain . . . '

'Exactly!' emphasised the Dutchman, thumping a fist into the palm of his other hand. 'Anyone can see that he's cracking up.'

'With respect, sir, you're not making it any easier for him.' There was more than a hint of criticism in the Chief's reply.

Van Lutyens resented this. 'That's not what I'm here for. I come to give professional advice – Mr Robson ignores it! He knows rigs, yes. He knows much about engineering, but not all. And it is obvious he knows nothing about the state of mind of those men out there on the rigs!'

The Chief replied without looking up. 'Mr Robson was out there a long time, sir.'

Van Lutyens sighed with frustration. He felt he was getting nowhere with either Harris or the Chief Engineer. 'Yes, it is true. Robson has great experience – of normal conditions. But these are not normal conditions. Something very strange is happening, but Robson refuses to accept the new factor, the unexplained factor.'

'So what do you think he should do?' asked Harris.

'I know exactly what *I* would do.' Van Lutyens hesitated briefly, then spoke directly. 'I would close the Compound and evacuate the rigs!'

The Chief exchanged a quick anxious glance with Harris. 'He'd never do it!'

'Can't you see, Chief?' argued the Dutchman. 'It's the only safe, logical thing to do until all this business is sorted out.' The Chief looked unconvinced. Van Lutyens continued: 'Look, we've lost contact with two of those rigs out at sea. We've got a major blockage in the main pipeline, a jammed impeller . . . we don't know what is causing all this trouble!'

Harris interrupted. 'But we regained contact with Baxter on Rig D. He said everything was under control.'

Exasperated, the Dutchman replied, 'And we haven't heard from him since! And what about Rig C? We've lost contact with them also.'

The Chief was beginning to run out of answers. 'It's probably a telecommunications fault somewhere,' he spluttered.

Van Lutyens pursued his point firmly. 'All right, so maybe it is. But my point is that we must at least check! Just as we must check the impeller valve at the base of the shaft. But Robson will do nothing! Nothing!'

Harris and the Chief Engineer looked at each other, clearly swayed by the Dutchman's argument.

'I suppose Robson might listen if we all put it to him,' suggested Harris. 'What do you think, Chief?'

'There's some sense in what Mr van Lutyens says, sir,' said the Chief, massaging the tense muscle in the back of his neck. 'We should check.'

The Dutchman sighed with relief. At last there was a glimmer of hope.

In the TARDIS, the Doctor, Victoria, and Jamie were looking at a sketched drawing of a Weed Creature which the Doctor had turned up on the page of a very large, old and dusty reference book. The drawing was identical to the Weed Creature Victoria had seen in the Oxygen Room at the Refinery: enormous bubbled tentacles emerging from a large mass of sea foam.

'That's it, Doctor!' explained Victoria, pointing nervously at the drawing. 'That's the same creature I saw!'

The Doctor looked subdued and concerned. 'Yes. I was afraid it might be.'

'But how did the picture get in this book?'

The Doctor was studying the drawing through a large magnifying glass. 'The book is a list of legends and superstitions. This particular drawing is based on legends supplied by ancient mariners in the North Sea, probably around the middle of the eighteenth century.'

Jamie was dumbfounded. 'You mean this drawing is the same as the creature Victoria saw in the Compound?'

The Doctor looked up at Jamie through the magnifying glass. It was a grotesque sight. 'I'm afraid so, Jamie.'

'And what about the clumps of weed?'

The Doctor put down the magnifying glass. 'I don't know. But there's obviously some connection between the weed and the creatures themselves . . .'

While the Doctor was speaking, Jamie's face suddenly started to curl. He was building up to a sneeze. '*Aah . . . aah . . .*'

Victoria looked anxiously first at the Doctor, then at Jamie. 'Jamie . . . Jamie, you're going to . . . to . . .'

'*Choo!*' Jamie's sneeze was deafening, and this was just the start. But before he could sneeze again, the Doctor suddenly yelled out frantically.

'Victoria! Look out!'

Victoria turned with a shocked start, to stare in horror at the seaweed specimen in the glass tank just behind her. It had grown to over double its size, its tentacles hanging menacingly over the edge of the tank, covered in white foam. And the thumping sound it made was like a human heartbeat.

Victoria screamed out loud just as the Doctor pulled her out of the way.

To everyone's amazement, the heartbeat sound stopped

81

abruptly, the seaweed vibrated, and immediately retreated back into the tank.

'Jamie!' shouted the Doctor. 'Put the top on!' He quickly helped Jamie to replace the cover which had been forced open on top of the glass tank. 'Turn off the gas – quick!'

Jamie turned off the cylinder taps, and the sound of hissing gas stopped immediately. But the TARDIS was filled with an unpleasant smell, which caused everyone to cough and splutter.

'I was right!' said the Doctor, covering his mouth and studying the seaweed specimen now lying dormant at the bottom of the glass tank. 'The seaweed formations are feeding off the natural gas beneath the North Sea. But the gas they're expelling is toxic.' He looked closer at the specimen. 'And why did this stuff suddenly retreat back into the tank? Hmm, I wonder . . . ' He straightened up, and made for the door. 'Come on! We have to move fast!'

'Where are we going?' asked Victoria, edging her way cautiously past the tank.

The Doctor had already opened the door and disappeared outside. But his voice could be heard calling, 'I want to take another look at Harris's place!'

The seaweed specimen remained quite still in its glass cage. After the Doctor, Jamie, and Victoria had gone, it began to throb with life again.

7

The Figure on the Beach

The Dutchman was clearly right about one thing. Robson was beginning to crack up.

'No, I will *not* listen!' yelled the Controller maniacally from the observation platform in the Control Hall. Everyone was watching him in astonishment: van Lutyens, Harris, Price, the Chief Engineer, the communications crew. 'It's you, van Lutyens, isn't it? Isn't it!' Robson leaned over the rail to the Dutchman, his face contorted with anger. 'You've been trying to undermine my authority ever since you came here! You and Harris. You've been stirring up trouble round here just to get at me, haven't you? Now you've got the Chief on your side . . . ' He suddenly turned his bitter outburst onto the Chief Engineer. 'One of my oldest and trusted . . . I thought at least I could trust you!'

The Chief looked crushed. 'Mr Robson, all we want you to do is to . . . '

'I *know* what you want me to do – all of you! Every part of Robson's body seemed to be trembling, and his eyes seemed twice their size. 'You want to see me give up, don't you?' He laughed scornfully. 'Well, you'll never get that pleasure because . . . because . . . ' He stopped to look around at all the anxious faces watching him. 'All of you . . . all against me! Very well, if that's the way you want it, go right ahead! Go and join *Mr* van Lutyens and his gang of academic friends!' He scrambled down from the platform to look van Lutyens straight in the face. 'Go on, join him! But just remember – I'm still in charge of this . . . I'm still . . . ' He stopped, squinted his eyes, and rubbed his forehead. But he quickly recovered and lashed out at the crew again. 'Get back to work! Get . . . What the hell are you all staring . . . ' He stopped again, then turned suddenly, and practically ran to the Compound entrance door.

For a brief moment after Robson's exit, everyone remained in stunned silence. Finally, van Lutyens spoke to Harris.

'Well?' said the Dutchman solemnly, 'You still think he's capable of running this place?'

Harris seemed in a state of shock. All he could do was to exchange a bewildered glance with the Chief, and shrug his shoulders indecisively. This irritated van Lutyens. There was nothing he despised more than someone who was unwilling to accept responsibility. 'All right!' he snapped. 'You can do what you like, but I'm getting in touch with my people in the Hague.'

'But what can they do?' asked Harris.

'I don't know. But at least they can push your people in London into some kind of action! That man, that fool – he is no longer sane!'

The Dutchman left Harris and the Chief deep in thought, unsure what to do. Then he hurried across to Price at the Control Cone and barked, 'Get me a direct line to Mr van der Post at Hague Central!'

Robson returned to his cabin and slammed the door behind him. He was thoroughly exhausted, drained of all energy. For a moment, he stood with his back leaning against the door, looking around his cabin. It was nothing more than a small, stark room, more like a ship's cabin than the living quarters of an Administrative Controller. But there was one human touch in the room. It was a small framed photograph on a cabinet beside Robson's bunk bed.

Robson pulled open his collar, wiped the sweat from his forehead, and crossed the room to take a look at the photograph. It was of an attractive young woman, Angie, Robson's wife, who had been killed in a car crash twenty-two years ago. Robson picked up the photograph and stared at it painfully. It was a time of his life that he would never forget, for, at the time of the accident, he himself had been driving the car in which Angie was the passenger.

Robson replaced the photograph, sighed deeply, then went and slumped down on his bunk, to stare aimlessly up at the ceiling.

In the corridor outside, someone was cautiously approaching the door of Robson's cabin. He was a sinister figure, small and fat, dressed in white cap, tunic, and trousers. It was Mr Oak, one of the two maintenance controllers. He moved silently, delicately, like a prowling cat in slow motion.

In his cabin, Robson's eyelids closed. He was finally succumbing to sleep.

Mr Oak had his ear pressed up against Robson's door. He could hear nothing, but knew what was going on. He smiled gently, and waited.

Robson sat up with a start, thinking he had heard a movement at the door. 'Who's there?' he yelled irritably. 'I'm not to be disturbed! Go away!'

With a broad grin on his face, Mr Oak reached down and turned the key in the door lock. Then he moved on to the *EMERGENCY VENT* Control Unit on the wall, and operated the switch to *OPEN*.

Robson was lying on his back again, eyes closed. For a moment or so he seemed to be relaxed, and falling into a deep sleep. Suddenly, his eyes sprang open, and were staring at the ceiling. He could hear a slight hum coming from

85

somewhere in the room. The sound stopped abruptly, to be replaced by other, more menacing sounds. The hissing of gas, the thumping, pulsating rhythms of a heartbeat. Robson's face was running with sweat, his eyes couldn't focus properly. He began to cough and splutter as the gas started to affect him. He tried to sit up, but was too weak, and slumped back onto the bunk again. All he could do now was lie there helplessly, struggling for breath, listening to the overpowering sound of the heartbeat. Gradually his eyes began to focus, then opened wide in horror, transfixed towards the ceiling.

The ventilation grille above Robson was wide open, and the first few blobs of white foam were beginning to appear.

Robson was struggling to move, but his entire body felt like marble, as though he were paralysed.

Soon, the blobs of white foam became a deluge, bursting open the grille with a loud crash.

Robson tried to shout out, but it was taking all his effort to even open his lips. Blobs of white foam were cascading down onto him.

The sound in the room was now deafening. Thumping. Pulsating. Bubbling. The heartbeat! Gradually, through the mass of white foam there emerged the long, curling tendrils of the Weed Creature, stretching down closer and closer towards Robson's face . . .

In the corridor outside, Harris was about to knock on the door of Robson's cabin. But he stopped dead as he heard Robson's piercing scream echoing out from inside the room.

'Mr Robson!' shouted Harris, banging on the door. 'Mr Robson, what is it? What's going on?'

'Help me!' Robson was calling frantically, banging on the other side of the door. 'Let me out of here!' He screamed again.

Harris desperately tried to open the door. It was locked. But the key was still in the lock, so he quickly turned it. No sooner had he done so than Robson pulled open the door. There were small blobs of white foam clinging to his clothes, and he was trembling with fear as he clutched his face. 'My face!' he spluttered. 'It touched my face!'

Harris was horrified. 'Mr Robson . . .' But Robson pushed him out of the way and rushed down the corridor in panic shouting, 'It touched my face!'

Harris called after him. 'Mr Robson! Wait! I need your permission to send two men down the impeller shaft . . .' He was wasting his time. Robson had disappeared through the door leading to the outer Compound area.

Harris, totally shocked and bewildered, brushed the lock of hair from his eye. Then he turned to look at the door of Robson's cabin, and cautiously went inside.

The sight that was awaiting Harris in Robson's cabin, was one which he would remember for the rest of his life. The moment he entered the room, he was coughing and spluttering from the deadly gas fumes which had almost overpowered Robson. There were blobs of bubbling white foam everywhere, and dangling down from the remains of the ventilator grille were the long, curling tendrils of the Weed Creature, its massive heartbeat pounding with frenzied, deafening life . . .

The short winter daylight was already giving way to the early evening darkness, as the Doctor, Jamie, and Victoria peered through the window into the Harrises' sitting-room. There was hardly a murmur of sound, only the rumbling of waves crashing onto the distant sea shore. Luckily the window was not locked, so the Doctor was able to climb into the room quite easily. Jamie and Victoria followed him in.

'Good!' whispered the Doctor, trying to see in the dark, 'Nobody around. Much better on our own.'

'Speak for yourself,' said Jamie apprehensively. He wasn't at all happy with the Doctor for bringing them back to such a place. 'I don't see why we can't just go back to the TARDIS and get out of here. This place is full of . . . of . . . ah . . . ah . . .' It was happening again. Jamie was about to sneeze.

'Jamie!' gasped Victoria. 'You're not going to . . . ' Even as she spoke, Jamie exploded into a fit of sneezing.

'Gas!' The Doctor covered his mouth immediately. 'Out of here – quick!'

The Doctor led the way out into the hall.

Victoria was covering her mouth with her sweater. 'Where's it coming from?'

'I don't know,' said the Doctor, looking up and down the hall. 'Jamie! Look in the kitchen!'

Jamie rushed off to the kitchen, leaving the Doctor and Victoria to find their way into the bedroom.

The Doctor opened the bedroom door, and looked in. The room was in darkness. 'Mrs Harris?' he called. 'Are you all right?'

No reply. There was an ominous silence in the room.

The Doctor fumbled for the light switch, and turned it on.

The air was immediately pierced by the thumping, heart-beat sound. Victoria screamed out hysterically for the floor was crawling with clumps of pulsating seaweed, their bubbled tendrils reaching out from the mass of white foam.

Coughing and spluttering, the Doctor threw his arms around Victoria to protect her. On the other side of the room, they were horrified to see that Maggie Harris was missing from the bed, where they had last seen her lying in a coma.

'Doctor!' Jamie was yelling at the top of his voice from the kitchen. 'Help me!'

The Doctor quickly slammed the bedroom door and locked it. Then he grabbed Victoria by the arm, and practically dragged her off down the hall.

'Jamie!' The Doctor burst into the kitchen to find his companion in real trouble. The patio door was wide open, and Jamie himself was balanced precariously on top of a table in the middle of the room. All around him, the floor was just like the bedroom, crawling with clumps of seaweed and foam, all pulsating with hideous life. And the same merciless, thumping heartbeat!

Jamie let out the most enormous sneeze. His eyes were streaming with tears from the gas fumes, and he was fighting for breath. 'Doctor! Do something! Get . . . get me out of here! But he seemed to be in an impossible situation, for he was completely isolated by the weed and foam which prevented his escape in any direction.

'Stay where you are, Jamie!' yelled the Doctor frantically. 'Hold on!'

As the Doctor was speaking, Victoria suddenly clasped here head, as if about to swoon. 'The pressure . . . Doctor . . . my head . . . ' She was struggling to breath. 'I can't stand . . . the pressure . . . '

The Doctor caught hold of Victoria just as she was on the point of collapse. 'No, Victoria!' He pulled her back into the hall, and shook her violently by the shoulders. 'Come on now, Victoria! Deep breath!' Victoria's head rolled from side to side as she struggled to revive. Gradually, her strength returned, and she was able to stand on her own two feet again. 'Good girl!' said the Doctor, patting Victoria's cheeks reassuringly with his hands. 'Now – quick! Help me!'

'Doctor!' Jamie's calls from the kitchen were becoming more desperate. 'Hurry . . . '

The Doctor returned to the kitchen door and shouted back. 'Hold on, Jamie! Hold on!' He rushed out into the hall again to look for something that would aid Jamie's escape. He settled on a pair of long curtains that were hanging up at the hall window. 'Help me, Victoria – quick!' With Victoria's help, he ripped down the curtains, and tied them together in a huge knot lengthways. 'Stay here!'

'Doctor . . . ' Jamie's voice was becoming weaker as he began to droop under the pressure of the toxic fumes and overpowering sound of the heartbeat.

'Don't let it beat you now, Jamie!' yelled the Doctor from the doorway. 'Wake up!'

Jamie did not reply. His body was gradually crumpling dangerously close to the edge of the table, where the weed tendrils were waiting for him.

This time the Doctor shouted as loud and as firmly as he could. 'Wake up, Jamie!' Jamie was sinking fast and could not respond. 'Do as I say!' yelled the Doctor. 'Wake up!' Jamie suddenly snapped back into life again, and rubbed his eyes. 'That's it, Jamie! That's it! Quick now! Take the other end!' The Doctor swung one end of the curtain round and round his head, and threw it across to Jamie who caught it at the first attempt. 'Tie it to the leg of the table, Jamie, Hurry!'

It was no easy task for Jamie to tie the end of the curtain to the table leg, for the seaweed clumps seemed determined to drag him down into the sea. But he was finally able to give a weak signal to the Doctor that he had secured the end of the curtain to the table leg.

'Right!' yelled the Doctor. 'Now hold on!'

The Doctor spit on both his hands, took hold of the other end of the curtain, and with all the strength he could muster, pulled the table with Jamie on it, inch by inch towards the door. It was a slow, tense movement, which seemed to provoke the seaweed clumps into a squealing rage. The more the table moved, the more their tendrils tried to reach up and curl themselves around Jamie's legs.

Finally, Jamie's ordeal came to an end. As soon as the table reached the open door the Doctor and Victoria dragged him from it, and supported him out into the hall.

'Let's get out of here!' yelled the Doctor, as the foam and weed rapidly overflowed into the hall after them, bubbling, pulsating, and squirming with aggressive life . . .

Harris looked around Robson's cabin in total disbelief. Only a few minutes earlier the place had been a mass of bubbling white foam, and the ventilator grille jammed with the enormous figure of the Weed Creature.

'But it was here I tell you,' said the bewildered Harris, his eyes darting to every corner of the room. 'I saw it!'

Van Lutyens was only partly sceptical. 'Did you?'

'It was trying to get into the room from the grille up there.

A huge, hideous creature with long tendrils . . . like a . . . like a gigantic octopus. It could move . . . it was alive . . . ' Van Lutyens ignored him. He was too busy looking around the room. 'You don't believe me, do you!' snapped Harris.

'On the contrary, my friend. I *do* believe you.' The Dutchman had found a few traces of white foam near the grille opening. It must have escaped through the ventilating system, just as it did in the Oxygen Store Room.'

'The Oxygen Room? You mean, when that girl – Victoria – when she was locked in?'

'Precisely.' Van Lutyens was standing on Robson's bunk, staring up into the grille opening. 'My theory is that when you saw it, it had already accomplished its purpose in this room, and was finding its way out again into the ventilator shaft.'

Harris turned to look at van Lutyens. He was puzzled. 'Accomplished its purpose? What purpose?'

'Who knows?' replied the Dutchman, rubbing some of the foam between his fingers. 'We know so little about this phenomenon, or whatever it is. The trouble is, nobody is even trying to find out. Least of all Mr Robson!'

'Robson is in no position to find out anything,' said Harris, tersely. 'He rushed out of this room as though he was out of his mind.'

'Did he now?' The Dutchman took a pointed interest in Harris's remark. 'Well, we'd better alert security. Robson may do himself some harm.'

Van Lutyens took a last look around the room, then left. Harris followed him out, and locked the door behind him. 'At least nothing's going to get out through *this* door,' said Harris efficiently.

The Dutchman shook his head in despair at Harris's feeble logic. 'My friend, there must be hundreds of ventilator grilles in this compound. If any of that foam is in the shaft, it could find its way out through any one of them.'

Harris looked crestfallen. Such a thought clearly hadn't entered his statistical mind. 'I suppose you're right,' he

91

sighed. 'In which case, we must ensure that all emergency ventilators are kept shut.'

Van Lutyens decided it was pointless trying to answer Harris. He just marched determinedly along the corridor, with Harris following close behind.

'I trust you now know what you must do?' said the Dutchman, striding on.

'Do?'

'You must exert your authority and take over the Compound.' Van Lutyens stopped at the transparent door leading to the Control Hall. He pressed a button on the wall, and the door slid open. Harris entered first, then the Dutchman.

'Price!' called Harris, going straight to the Control Cone. 'I want you to alert all security posts. Mr Robson may be ill. I'd like to know his whereabouts.'

'Very good, sir!' Price acknowledged Harris's order, then turned back to the Control Console to carry it out.

Harris continued, displaying a gradual confidence in his own authority. 'And instruct all areas to keep their emergency air vent systems closed.'

Price swung a puzzled look at Harris.

'Do you understand?' asked Harris firmly. 'Then get on with it!'

'Yes, sir!' Price turned back again to the Console.

Van Lutyens was impressed. 'You're taking over then?' he asked, walking with Harris to the office area.

Harris lowered his eyes almost guiltily before replying. 'Mr Robson's still officially in charge.'

'I have to remind you, Harris,' said the Dutchman, 'that I have already informed my own authorities in the Hague. As far as I am concerned, it is now up to you to do the same with London.'

Harris stopped walking, and brushed the lock of hair from his eye. He hesitated a moment, tense and unsure what to do. His instinct was telling him that what van Lutyens was asking him to do was something that should have been done several days ago. 'Yes,' he said, deep in thought, 'you're right.' He looked across the Hall to the Control Cone and called, 'Price!'

Price turned quickly, and called back. 'Sir!'

'Get me Board Headquarters in London. I want to speak to Megan Jones.'

The Doctor, Jamie, and Victoria were making their way along one of the Compound corridors leading to the Control Hall. Jamie was still feeling queasy after his rescue from the foam and seaweed clumps in Harris's quarters.

'Take it easy now, Jamie,' said the Doctor, clearly worried about Jamie's condition. 'What you need is a few hours' sleep.'

'Aye,' said Jamie weakly. 'I wouldn'a mind so much, but I feel so . . . so dizzy . . . ' He stumbled, leaving the Doctor and Victoria to support him.

'It's all right, Jamie,' said the Doctor, 'Just rest a moment.'

Jamie was panting hard. 'Aye. Just need to get my breath back.' He straightened up, and leaned his back up against the corridor wall.

Victoria leaned against the wall too. She was looking very depressed. 'Oh, Doctor, why is it that we always seem to land up in trouble?'

The Doctor smiled affectionately. 'Spice of life, my dear.'

'I'm not so sure,' Victoria said with a deep sigh. 'I don't really enjoy being scared out of my wits every second.'

The Doctor turned to give her an anxious look. 'Victoria? Is something wrong?'

'Wrong!' snapped Victoria tensely. . 'After all that's happened in this . . . this terrible place!' She suddenly realised that the Doctor was showing concern for her. 'I'm sorry, Doctor,' she said guiltily. 'I'm perfectly all right - really. It's just that I . . . well, I wish I . . . oh, never mind.'

The Doctor watched Victoria with concern as she strolled

off aimlessly along the corridor ahead of them. He was puzzled by the mood she was in. Even Jamie noticed Victoria's odd behaviour. He had never seen her quite like this before.

At the Control Cone, Harris was finishing off a video conversation with Megan Jones at Board Headquarters in London. The woman on the central monitor screen was a redhead, in her late forties, and attractive in a hard sort of way.

'Thank you, Miss Jones,' said Harris, talking directly into the audio feed built into the monitor. 'We'll see you in three hours' time.' The woman nodded without smiling, and the screen went blank. Harris paused anxiously, then turned to van Lutyens. 'In three hours' time the whole compound will be crawling with Board Officials.'

Van Lutyens shrugged his shoulders. 'Let's hope that by then the situation hasn't got any worse.'

The two men walked together towards the observation platform. As they went, their conversation was of particular interest to a couple of crewmen who were listening from a shadowy corner near the Compound Exit door. It was Mr Oak and Mr Quill.

'I only hope Megan Jones understands why I've taken over,' said Harris. 'It was she who insisted that Robson should run this particular complex in the early days.'

The Dutchman gave Harris a comforting pat on the back. 'Stop worrying. You did what you have to do. You couldn't have let Robson go on ignoring the situation here. It would be criminal to take any more chances with the men out there on those rigs. Their safety is now the responsibility of someone far more superior than you.'

Harris and van Lutyens climbed the few steps up to the observation platform, and paused briefly to glance up at the pipeline tube.

'If only we knew what it is we're up against,' sighed Harris. 'These creatures that have been getting into the Refinery. Where do they come from?'

94

In the shadows nearby, Mr Oak and Mr Quill exchanged a satisfied smile.

'Even worse,' continued Harris, 'we don't know what the devil they actually are . . . '

'That's where you're wrong, Mr Harris!'

Everyone in the Hall turned. It was the Doctor's voice booming out from the other side of the Communications Area. Jamie and Victoria were with him.

'We *do* know what the creatures are.' The Doctor hurried across to Harris and van Lutyens at the observation platform. 'At least I *think* I know what they are. Seaweed!'

Van Lutyens was first to react. 'Seaweed?'

'A somewhat different species to what you'd normally expect to find on the beach.' The Doctor's head didn't move, but his eyes stared straight up at Harris and van Lutyens on the platform. 'This particular type of weed happens to be dangerously alive.'

There was a stunned silence throughout the Hall. All eyes were turned towards the Doctor.

'Alive?' Harris's response was hardly more than a whisper. 'But how can . . . '

'I think you'd better listen to me,' warned the Doctor. He turned to address everyone in the Hall. 'All of you!' He paused, looked around the anxious faces, and continued. 'Large formations of seaweed are drifting onto the beach somewhere along this coastline. Seaweed that shows clear signs of containing living organisms similar to that of a human being.'

There were murmurs of shock and disbelief all around.

'Did I hear you right?' called the Chief Engineer from the open door of the impeller area. 'You're saying it's this seaweed that's blocking the pipeline?'

'Yes I am!' the Doctor called back. 'In my opinion there's no doubt about it.'

'I knew it!' yelled the Dutchman excitedly. 'I knew it all the time! There is no time to lose. We must clear the base of the impeller shaft immediately . . . '

'No - wait!' The Doctor stopped van Lutyens from rushing off towards the impeller area. 'The weed is capable of protecting itself.'

'Protecting itself?' Harris was more confused than ever.

The Doctor started pacing up and down, half-talking to himself. 'As far as I can make out, the weed is some kind of a parasite that emits a toxic gas. It attaches itself to other living things . . . ' He stopped pacing, and looked back at Harris and van Lutyens. 'And that, gentlemen, includes human beings.'

In the shadows nearby, Mr Oak and Mr Quill slipped out quietly through the Compound Exit door.

Harris was now on the verge of panic. He rushed down the platform steps, and went straight to the Doctor. 'Doctor. What happens to human beings when this parasite weed attaches itself?'

The Doctor's response was a solemn one. 'I'm afraid I don't know that yet, Mr Harris.'

'But my wife was stung by the seaweed.'

'Yes, but she appeared to survive. How is she now?'

'I asked the Medicare Matron to bring her in.' He turned to Price at the Control Cone and called, 'Get Medicare for me! Ask them what condition my wife is in!'

'Yes, sir!' Price turned back to the Control Console.

Harris walked with the Doctor to join Jamie and Victoria. He lowered his voice as he spoke. 'Doctor. I saw one of these creature things that your friend Victoria saw in the Oxygen Room.'

The Doctor swung Harris a startled look. 'You did? Where?'

'In Mr Robson's cabin. It might have attacked him - I don't know. But he was in a wild state when I went to see him. He just rushed out of the room like a madman, and hasn't been seen since.'

'Oh, dear . . . ' The Doctor was disguising his worst fears.

'Mr Harris!' Price was calling from the Control Cone.

Harris called back. 'What is it?'

'Sir, Matron says she's sorry, but she hasn't brought your wife in yet. She's sending someone over to your quarters now.'

The Doctor turned suddenly in alarm and called to Price, 'What was that you said?'

'What is it, Doctor?' asked Harris, sensing the Doctor's anxiety. 'What's wrong?'

'Mr Harris, we've just come from your quarters. Your wife wasn't there.'

'Aye,' added Jamie breathlessly, 'and the place was crawling with that foam and seaweed stuff!'

Harris's face looked like white marble, and his lips turned blue. 'Is this true?' he asked the Doctor.

The Doctor frowned and replied gravely, 'I'm afraid so.'

'Then where is she? What's happened to her?'

Harris was now beside himself with fear and apprehension. But the Doctor's response could only be a helpless shrug of the shoulders.

Van Lutyens came forward to try and offer some logical explanation to Harris for his wife's disappearance. 'Harris, I'm sure you'll find that – '

'Out of my way!' snapped Harris, as he pushed the Dutchman aside and rushed out of the Hall. Everyone watched him go in stunned, helpless silence.

'What *has* happened to Mrs Harris?' Van Lutyens asked the Doctor. 'Is it something to do with the seaweed creatures?'

The Doctor lowered his head, covered his eyes, and replied gravely, 'I don't know. I just don't know . . . '

The sky was clear now, and in the twilight the first star of night was already visible to the naked eye. The sunset had bequeathed a dark, crimson glow along the vast thin line of the horizon. The ripples on the waves were glistening like rubies, disguising the endless fronds of seaweed and foam that were drifting in on the evening tide. The afternoon thaw had dispersed most of the thin blanket of snow covering the surrounding hills, and on the beach the small pools of seawater were edged with the first signs of a hard frost.

The beach was totally deserted but for the solitary figure of a woman. She was nothing more than a silhouette against the fading twilight, standing by the water's edge, her gaze transfixed out to sea. There were small formations of hair-like weed growing on her neck, face, and hands.

The woman was Maggie Harris.

As the ice-cold waves pounded onto the shoreline, and the foam and weed gathered into one vast mass, Maggie became aware that someone was approaching her from along the beach. She did not turn to look. It was as though she knew who or what to expect. The sound of footsteps crunching on shingles came to a halt right beside her. She did not turn to look. 'There is little time,' said Maggie. Her voice was eerily soft and controlled. 'You know what you must do.'

'Yes.' The voice that replied was that of a man.

'You will obey?' asked Maggie.

The man nodded without speaking. It was Robson. He looked tired, his face drained of all blood. Like Maggie, he was obviously under the 'control' of some unseen force.

Both were now staring out to sea. They were oblivious to the biting cold and icy spray from the tide that was lapping perilously close to their feet. Only one thought dominated their minds. It was the gradual approach of the thumping, heartbeat sound.

Maggie spoke again. 'It is time for me to go. You will stay.'

The thumping sound was becoming louder and louder, closer and closer.

Maggie did not speak again. She and Robson remained as still as marble, their lifeless eyes transfixed towards the open, darkening sea. Their mission now was to wait.

The thumping sound was reaching a crescendo. Then suddenly, as if commanded by a signal, Maggie started to move. Slowly, methodically, she began to wade into the oncoming tide. The water was now seething with foam, and the mass of weed was wriggling with impatient anticipation.

Robson, under complete control now, stared impassively out to sea.

Maggie was wading deeper and deeper into the foam. Her eyes were transfixed mesmerically out to the wide expense of ocean. Soon, the foam was above her waist, then her shoulders. But still she did not, could not, stop.

It took only a few moments for Maggie to disappear beneath the surface of the water, which was engulfed by the deadly weed and foam. And as she went, the thumping, heartbeat sound became a squeal, a shriek of triumph, echoing across the beach and hills.

Robson remained quite still. For him, the night had only just begun.

8

The Impeller Shaft

'Rig D . . . Rig D . . . Control calling Rig D. Come in, please!' There was a note of desperation in Price's voice as he tried to restore video contact with Rig D out at sea. But the central monitor screen at the Control Cone remained stubbornly blank. Price turned to van Lutyens and the Doctor, who were anxiously watching the screen. 'I'm sorry, sir. I can't raise them.'

The Dutchman rubbed his chin despondently. 'Try Rig A again.'

Price shook his head. 'I've been trying them ever since first light this morning, sir. That's three of the rigs not answering now.'

Van Lutyens was in a quandary. Robson had vanished, and Harris had rushed off in a panic to look for his wife. If someone in authority didn't soon take action, the morale of the men out on the remaining rigs was going to crack. He turned to Price again, who was waiting for further orders. 'Try the Guard Posts again. See if there is any sign of Mr Harris.'

'Yes, sir!' Price turned back to the Control Console.

Van Lutyens, deep in thought, moved off slowly towards the office Area. The Doctor walked with him.

'Three rigs now,' said the Dutchman gravely, 'with absolutely no contact with them whatsoever. Something's happened to them, I just know it.'

'Can't you send someone out to investigate?' suggested the Doctor.

'Unfortunately, I have no authority. I am here purely as a technical adviser. Harris is in charge now. When he comes back he must authorise the Company helicopter to go out and take a look at the rigs.'

As they reached the office Area, van Lutyens stopped and turned. He was looking up at the pipeline tube curling around the Communications Hall.

'Are you absolutely certain there's nothing we can do?' asked the Doctor.

'Nothing,' replied the Dutchman pessimistically. 'All we can do is to sit – and wait.'

In the Impeller Area, the Chief Engineer was also staring up at the pipeline tube. It was an abomination to him that the impeller – *his* impeller – was being silenced by forces beyond his control. The safe running of the Refinery impeller had preoccupied the Chief's life for so many years now. To many, he *was* the impeller. They called him the 'Chief' mainly because few even knew his real name.

The Chief's crewmen were just as despondent. They were lounging around aimlessly, some squatting on the floor, some standing with hands in pockets, others nodding off from sheer exhaustion.

The deadly silence was to be short-lived.

Everyone suddenly sprang into life and turned to look at the surface of the shaft. Their blood was chilled with terror. It was the sound again. *That* sound. Thumping. Pulsating. Somewhere down below, in the dark bowels of the impeller shaft . . .

*   *   *

Jamie and Victoria were back in the crew cabin they had first been taken to after their capture by the Refinery Security Guards. Jamie was half asleep on the upper bunk, but Victoria was sitting on the edge of the lower bunk, deep in agonising thought.

Victoria sighed, and finally spoke. 'Jamie?'

There was no reply. In his dream, Jamie was playing his bagpipes on the banks of some windswept Highland loch. But his snores were not exactly musical.

'Jamie!' Victoria stood up and glared at Jamie. 'Are you asleep?'

Jamie's eyes sprang open, but they were glazed with sleep. 'Huh? Och no,' he groaned with a wide yawn, 'just resting ma eyes.'

'I don't know how you can just drop off like that with all this trouble going on.'

'Stop worrying will ye,' complained Jamie, his eyelids having great difficulty in remaining open. 'The Doctor's bound to come up with some sort of solution. He always does.' He curled up, and turned his back on her.

'Yes,' said Victoria, half to herself. She was in a strange, tormented mood again. 'But what then?'

'How d'you mean, ''what then?'' '

'I mean, where will we go the next time?'

Jamie turned over again. It was clear that Victoria was not going to let him have his sleep. 'You know better than to ask a daft question like that! We never know where we're going to end up. That's the fun of it.'

'Is it?' Victoria's large blue eyes were staring up at Jamie. They looked distant, and sad.

Jamie sat upright. He was concerned about Victoria. Ever since they first met, she'd been like a sister to him. They often knew what each other was thinking without actually puting it into words. But this was different. Just lately, Victoria had been showing no enthusiasm for her travels in the TARDIS. 'What's the matter, Victoria?' asked Jamie, looking his companion straight in the eyes with his

102

inimitable reassuring smile. 'You've been behaving strange ever since – '

'It's nothing.' Victoria moved away quickly. 'It doesn't matter.'

'You'll only worry the Doctor if you keep on . . . '

'Oh, for goodness sake, I said it didn't matter!' Victoria had turned her back on Jamie, and was glaring tensely out of the porthole window.

Jamie watched Victoria with a mixture of incredulity and anxiety. This was not the Victoria he knew. Something was very wrong.

Victoria turned from the window. She was consumed with guilt. 'I'm sorry, Jamie. I didn't mean to . . . go back to sleep – please.'

Jamie took a moment or so to believe her apologetic smile. Then he reluctantly settled back on his bunk again. 'Aye. Well don't you go worrying about that silly old weed,' he said. 'The Doctor will think of something.'

'Will he?' Victoria was gazing aimlessly out through the window again. So many questions were pulverising her thoughts. The weed grows, feeds off natural gas. But how fast does it grow, and what happens to those people who are physically touched by it? Victoria's innermost fears suddenly took on a horrifying reality. 'Jamie,' she said, turning quickly. 'I'm so frightened . . . '

Jamie was fast asleep, and snoring majestically. Victoria came across to the bunk, and glared at him. At first she was annoyed to be ignored, but as she watched him lying there with a look of perfect peace on his face, she couldn't resist an affectionate smile. To Victoria, Jamie was a very special person, the sort of brother everyone should have.

Suddenly, Victoria turned with a shocked gasp. Someone had entered the room behind her. 'Oh, it's you . . . ' she said, sighing with relief.

'Sorry, Victoria,' said the Doctor, closing the door. 'Did I startle you? Ah!' He went straight to look at Jamie, whose snores now sounded like a Highland reel. 'Well, he certainly needed some sleep. In fact, we all need some . . . ' He stretched his arms, and yawned.

Victoria sat down again on the edge of the lower bunk. 'Doctor,' she asked solemnly. 'What do you think is going on in this terrible place?'

The Doctor went to look out through the porthole window. 'I'm not sure, Victoria. I'm not sure at all.' He squinted as the early morning sun beamed across his tired face. 'It all looks so peaceful out there.'

Victoria waited a moment, then said, 'I heard that noise again. It was in the pipeline tube.'

The Doctor turned from the window, and nodded. 'Yes. I know. So did I.'

'Are they doing anything about it?'

'No. We have to wait.'

'*Wait!*' Victoria snapped. 'Wait for what? For that awful Weed Creature to come and attack us all?'

'Now, now, Victoria.' The Doctor immediately sensed Victoria's tension. He left the window, and went to sit beside her on the lower bunk. 'It's not as bad as that, you know.'

'Isn't it?' Victoria was not reassured. 'Even you don't really know how bad it is, do you? Come on now, Doctor, tell the truth – do you?'

The Doctor hesitated, then lowered his eyes uneasily. 'Well . . . not exactly – no.' He quickly looked up at Victoria for her reaction.

Victoria covered her eyes with her hands. She was clearly unnerved by the Doctor's uncertainty. 'Every time we go somewhere, something awful happens. Cybermen, Daleks, Yeti – all sorts of horrible things.' She turned to look at him. There was a pleading look in her eyes. 'Why can't we ever go where there's no fighting, no wars – just peace and happiness?'

The Doctor put his arm around Victoria, and she gently rested her head on his shoulder. 'My dear child,' said the Doctor reflectively. 'I'd take you there tomorrow – if I knew such a place existed.'

*   *   *

The beach was shrouded in a thin film of grey mist. The early morning sun was doing its best to penetrate the mist, and there were signs that within an hour or so it was going to turn out to be a fine, crisp winter's day.

Harris's feet were crunching on the shingles. He was well wrapped up against the bitter cold. Only his face was visible beneath the heavy Euro-Gas Company issue anorak. He came to a halt near the water's edge, and called out, 'Maggie! Where are you?' His voice sounded dull and lifeless in the frosty mist. For a few moments, he just stood there in the silence, waiting, hoping for a response to his call. Nothing. He tried again. 'Maggie! Maggie, where . . . are . . . you?' Again nothing, only the sound of gentle waves breaking onto the shingles. But as he slowly turned, a slight breeze caused the mist to twirl, and as it did so, Harris could just glimpse the outline of a human figure standing at the water's edge, only a short distance away from him. 'Maggie!' he called excitedly. 'Darling!' He rushed toward the figure. But it was not his wife. It was a man.

The man was Robson.

Harris was shocked. 'Mr Robson! What are you doing out here, sir?'

Robson did not reply. He was staring out to sea, a smile of calm and contentment on his face. It was almost as though he was mesmerised by the sounds coming from the depths of the ocean beyond.

Harris placed himself right in front of Robson, looking straight into his eyes. 'Sir, you have no coat on. You'll catch your death of cold.'

Robson still did not reply. His eyes were focussed through Harris rather than at him. He also looked older, and his hair was streaked with grey. That was something Harris hadn't noticed before.

Harris tried again. 'Mr Robson. Have you seen my wife?'

This time Robson did reply. But his voice was unnaturally quiet, almost inaudible. And his gaze was still bland, his thought-patterns controlled from elsewhere. 'Your wife?'

Harris stared at him eagerly. 'I've been searching all night for her. Please Mr Robson, if you've seen her . . . '

'You *will* find her, Mr Harris.' Robson's voice sounded stilted, almost robotic. And he made no effort to even look at Harris. 'You will soon be with her.'

'Are you sure you haven't seen her?' asked Harris desperately. But again Robson didn't reply. He just turned away, and walked off along the beach. Harris watched him go in disbelief, then called after him. 'Mr Robson!'

Robson never looked back. The last Harris saw of him was a silhouetted figure disappearing back into the grey, frosty mist that was now folding itself back in layers along the entire stretch of shoreline.

Back at the Refinery, van Lutyens was preparing to go down the impeller shaft. The Doctor and Jamie were tying a rope around his waist, whilst the Dutchman himself was checking the gas mask hanging around his neck.

'If you don't mind my saying Mr van Lutyens,' said the Doctor, testing the huge knot he had just tied in the Dutchman's rope, 'this is a very bad idea of yours. You don't know what you're up against.'

'Aye,' Jamie agreed, 'you wouldna' get me down there!'

'Thank you for your advice, gentlemen,' replied the Dutchman determinedly, 'but I must handle this my way.'

'With respect, sir,' said the Chief Engineer, pushing his way through the group of crewmen who were waiting anxiously by the impeller shaft, 'don't you think we should wait until Mr Harris comes back?'

The Dutchman shook his head. 'No, Chief. The only way to find out if this seaweed of yours is blocking the base of the shaft, is to go down there.'

'But you can't go alone, sir.'

The Dutchman hesitated, then turned to look back at the Chief. 'Will you send some of your men with me?'

The Chief was taken aback. He looked around the group

of anxious faces. They were dreading his reply. 'I couldn't do that, sir. Not without official approval.' The men breathed a sigh of relief.

The Dutchman grinned cynically. 'Thank you, Chief. Then let's get on with it, shall we?'

Two engineers helped him onto the lift platform. The two men were not dressed like the others. They were wearing white caps, jackets, and gloves. It was Mr Oak and Mr Quill.

'You know, I wish you wouldn't do this, Mr van Lutyens,' said the Doctor uneasily.

The Dutchman tested the strength of the rope tied around his waist. 'Just make sure you keep a firm hold on this rope. If anything goes wrong down there, I rely on you to pull me up.' He nodded to the two engineers. Mr Quill closed the safety rail, then Mr Oak pushed the operating button. Immediately a low humming sound was heard, and the lift started to move.

The Doctor and Jamie exchanged a sceptical, worried look, as they watched the indomitable figure of van Lutyens in the open lift, gradually disappearing out of view, down into the darkness of the impeller shaft . . .

The huge vertical shaft was a cold and eerie place, running parallel to the giant impeller itself, and extending deep into the bowels of the earth beneath the Refinery. Near the surface, small oval windows were cut into the circular metallic walls, but these were used mainly to check for any possible fractures in the pipeline tube. The only light available was that filtering down from the surface, and despite the air-conditioning system in the shaft, the air was thick and stifling.

Slowly, the lift platform descended to the base of the shaft, its passenger light casting a lattice of shadows around the metallic walls. Van Lutyens stood there alone, staring up at the anxious faces that were peering down at him from the surface, dreading what might be waiting for him below. As the lift eased deeper and deeper into the earth, he felt as though he was drowning, his whole life dancing before him.

Suddenly, the lift came to an abrupt halt. It had reached its final destination, the base of the shaft.

Van Lutyens paused a moment, and took one last look up at the group of faces peering down at him from the surface. They were now no more than a small blob of blurred light. Then he raised the lift's safety rail, turned on his torch, and stepped out onto a narrow metal ledge which completely encircled the walls of the shaft.

Without the pulverising sound of the giant impeller, the shaft seemed to be simmering with dark secrets, bathed in an unnatural silence. Every step that the Dutchman took sent echoes reverberating around the huge metallic cylinder.

Van Lutyens moved slowly, cautiously. The beam from his electronic torch darted from one part of the wall to another. So far so good. Everything just as it should be. At least, that's the way it looked. He moved on.

Eventually, the Dutchman's torch found what it was searching for. The beam fell onto a steel airlock door in the floor of the shaft, which gave access to the pipeline tube beneath the Refinery.

Climbing down from the inspection ledge, van Lutyens placed his torch on the floor, and slowly started turning the airlock wheel. It moved stubbornly, with a metallic grating sound that sent piercing echoes around the cylindrical walls.

As soon as he was satisfied that the wheel was fully unlocked, van Lutyens took a deep breath, and using all his strength, gradually pulled open the door. He paused a moment and listened. Complete silence. He stooped down to peer through the open door in the floor. Pitch dark. Not a sound. He picked up his torch again, and directed its beam down into the chamber beneath.

The horror was immediate. The eerie silence suddenly exploded into a cacophony of frenzied sound. It was the heartbeat. Thumping. Pulsating. The entire shaft area was vibrating. Van Lutyens was paralysed with fear. By the light of his torch he stared in terror at the cataclysmic sight beneath him. The entire pipeline chamber was engulfed in a seething, shapeless mass of seaweed formations, all pulsating, thumping, squealing in a surge of white bubbling foam. It was a nightmare vision, a breeding ground for an alien life-force from the dark depths of the ocean. It was a colony of devils!

'Van Lutyens . . . ' The Doctor's voice echoed down the lift shaft, but it had to compete with the awesome sound of the alien heartbeat.

'Doctor!' Van Lutyens yelled back frantically, but in his panic to escape, he dropped his torch and the beam went out, plunging the shaft into darkness again. He leapt up quickly, and tried to scramble back onto the inspection ledge. But it was too late. He started to cough and splutter. There was a hissing sound, and the smell of gas filled the shaft. He turned quickly, to look back over his shoulder. Even in the dark he could see it, the shapeless form of a massive Weed Creature, rising up from the foam, hissing deadly gas fumes, its tendrils slowly snaking their way towards van Lutyens.

Van Lutyens made one last attempt to climb up onto the inspection ledge. But the creature's tendrils were on him, wrapping themselves around his ankles, pulling him back towards the foam.

The Dutchman only had time to scream once.

Van Lutyens's scream sent a cold chill of terror amongst the group waiting at the surface of the lift shaft.

'Get him up!' yelled the Chief Engineer. The tension had drained all the blood from his face.

Mr Oak pressed the lift operating button. A humming sound was heard, and the lift started its slow ascent to the surface.

'Doctor, what is it? What's happened?' Victoria had entered the Impeller Area.

'It's van Lutyens, the Dutchman,' said Jamie gloomily. 'He's down there.'

Victoria went to the edge of the shaft and looked down at the approaching lift. 'What's happened to him?'

The Doctor was clearly expecting the worst. 'We don't know, Victoria.'

The lift finally reached the surface, and came to a stop with a dull thud. Everyone gathered round to look inside. It was empty.

'He's still down there,' said the Chief in despair. Mr Oak and Mr Quill exchanged a brief smile.

'Well, we can't just leave him there!' The Doctor was irritated with the Chief's casual acceptance of the emergency.

'What are we going to do, Doctor?' asked Jamie.

The Doctor's reply was firm and decisive. 'We're going down there!'

Jamie mouth dropped open wide in horror. '*You* may be, but I'm no'!'

'Jamie!' The Doctor turned to Jamie with one of those cunning smiles that he usually reserved for gentle persuasion. 'You surely wouldn't let me go down that shaft on my own – would you?'

Jamie was adamant. 'Look, Doctor, if you think I'm going to – ' He stopped, hesitated, then sighed deeply. 'Och! Come on then!'

The Doctor grinned, patted Jamie on the back affectionately, then got into the lift. Jamie followed him.

'Doctor, you can't do this,' said Victoria anxiously. 'You don't know what's down there. You can't go!'

The Doctor closed the safety rail. 'Don't worry, Victoria. We'll be back. That's a promise.'

Mr Oak pressed the operating button, and the lift rumbled down the shaft.

Harris entered the Communications Hall. After searching all night for Maggie, he looked tired, drawn, unshaven, and numb from the cold.

Price turned from the Control Cone. 'Mr Harris! We've been looking all night for you.' He was shocked by Harris's appearance. 'Are you all right, sir?'

110

Harris didn't reply, but asked wearily, 'Is there any news of my wife?'

'I'm afraid not, sir. You mean, you didn't find her?'

Harris shook his head.

Price was genuinely shocked. He knew how much Harris and his wife adored each other. Theirs was one of the few truly successful and devoted married relationships on the Compound. 'I'm very sorry, sir.'

Harris rubbed his tired eyes, and squinted at the TV monitor. 'What's happening?'

Price frowned. 'Megan Jones, sir.'

'What about her?'

'She's just arrived from Headquarters in London. She and her secretary have just passed through the outer perimeter gate. They'll be here any minute.'

Harris suddenly came to life. 'Let me know the moment she gets here!' he snapped brusquely. 'Where's Mr van Lutyens?'

'I believe he's in the Impeller Area, sir. Something terrible seems to have happened.'

'What's going on here?' All the impeller engineers turned to look at Harris, who was yelling from the doorway.

'Mr Harris!' There was a clear note of relief in the Chief Engineer's voice. 'Thank goodness you're back, sir.'

Harris came striding across to meet the Chief at the shaft. 'Where's Mr van Lutyens?'

'He went down the shaft, sir.'

'He *what?*'

'He wanted to find out what's blocking the pipeline.'

Harris glared at the Chief with incredulity. 'Where is he now?'

The Chief rubbed his mouth nervously with the back of his hand. 'He hasn't come back, sir. The Doctor and the boy have gone down after him . . . '

Harris exploded with anger as he had never done before. 'You fool! You stupid fool! Don't you know what you've done?' He quickly turned from the Chief, and yelled at Mr

111

Oak and Mr Quill, who were waiting by the lift shaft controls. 'Get them up at once!' Mr Oak and Mr Quill were bewildered by Harris's outburst. 'Did you hear what I said?' Harris yelled again. 'Stop that lift!'

Mr Oak was galvanised into action. But as he turned to push the lift operating button, the humming sound of the lift's descent came to an abrupt halt. Mr Oak hesitated, then after exchanging a faint, wry smile with Mr Quill, turned to Harris and said apologetically, 'I'm sorry, sir. It's too late.'

At the bottom of the impeller shaft, the Doctor and Jamie found themselves plunged into darkness – and silence. For a moment they remained in the lift, without moving, without saying a word. All they could do was to listen.

Jamie was first to speak. It was no more than a whisper. 'Why do I let you talk me into these things? We canna see a hand in front of us.'

The Doctor tried hard to sound confident. 'Nothing to worry about, Jamie. Just follow me.' He opened the safety rail and stepped out. Jamie followed close behind.

Like the Dutchman before them, their feet echoed on a metallic surface. The air was thick and clammy.

'Watch your step now,' warned the Doctor. 'We're on the inspection ledge. The pipeline chamber should be somewhere directly beneath us.'

Within a few moments, they had succeeded in climbing down from the ledge. Step by precarious step, they edged their way towards the airlock in the middle of the floor.

'Aaaaah . . . !' Jamie suddenly leapt back with a gasp.

'Jamie! What is it?'

Jamie was shivering. 'I – I don't know. I've just kicked something . . . on the floor . . . ' Cautiously, he stooped down and searched the floor blindly with his hand. Eventually, he found the object. 'It's a torch,' he said. 'Must be van Lutyens's.'

'Yes,' said the Doctor, his eyes desperately trying to pierce

112

the darkness. 'But where is he?' He moved away a few steps, then called back. 'Over here, Jamie! Shine the torch!'

Jamie tried to switch on the torch. 'Och! It's no good. The stupid thing's broken.'

The Doctor was crawling about on his hands and knees in the dark. 'I think I've found the door to the pipeline chamber. It's wide open!'

Jamie didn't like this at all. The dark made him feel far too vulnerable. 'Doctor, let's get out of here,' he called nervously. 'I've got a feeling there's something evil down here.'

'It all seems quiet enough to me, Miss Jones.' This earth-shattering observation came from Ronald Perkins, secretary to Megan Jones, Chairperson of the Refinery Board. He was an effete young man, a devoted, ambitious civil servant, who would sooner die than contradict his superiors.

'Of course it's quiet, Perkins,' said the Chairperson, who, together with Perkins, was being accompanied by an armed Security Guard along a corridor, on the way to the Communications Hall. 'Robson's an efficient man. That's why I gave him control of this Refinery. He knows the job backwards.'

'Then why the sudden panic?'

'I don't know. Young Harris was rather vague about what's going on here.'

'Vague? He said he was taking over from Robson. I wouldn't call that vague!' The moment he finished speaking, Perkins wished he could have bitten his tongue. He had made a fatuous remark.

The Chairperson came to a halt immediately. Perkins did likewise. Also the Security Guard. Megan Jones was an attractive middle-aged woman. She was born in the Rhondda Valley, the daughter of a coal-miner, but for reasons best known to herself, had decided to disguise her appealing Welsh accent in favour of a more affected London boardroom brogue. 'Perkins,' she said quietly, gently arranging her vivid red hair, 'you haven't met Robson, have you?'

'No.'

The Chairperson smiled. 'No. Well, I think when you do you will realise that he isn't the sort of man one pushes around.'

Perkins did his best to look intelligent. It was a difficult task. 'Then what's all this about?'

'Probably nothing more than just an internal squabble. Harris is a bright boy. I sent him down here to Robson because I thought he might benefit from Robson's practical experience. Obviously they just haven't hit it off.'

Perkins straightened his carefully knotted tie. 'But what was all that panic about the Refinery being in danger?'

The Chairperson's smile became more fixed. She never liked being cross-examined by anyone, let alone Perkins. 'Don't get carried away by Harris's hysterics, Perkins.'

Perkins was beginning to blush. 'All I meant was, if there's no panic, why did we – I mean – why did *you* have to come rushing down here like this?'

The Chairperson took a deep, bored sigh. 'We came down here, Perkins, to referee a battle between two clever men, neither of whom the Company can afford to lose.'

'In other words, we're pouring oil? Politics?'

The Chairperson smiled condescendingly at her secretary. 'That's my guess, Perkins. Anyway, let's go and see shall we?'

Perkins smiled back weakly at his superior, then quickly followed her along the corridor.

In the impeller area, there was an atmosphere of quiet desperation. Victoria, Harris, the Chief Engineer and all his crewmen were staring down into the darkness of the lift shaft, anxiously awaiting a sign from the Doctor and Jamie that they were safe.

'Isn't there any way we can get them up?' asked Harris. His voice was echoing down the shaft as he spoke.

The Chief shook his head. 'We daren't bring the lift up in case they want to get back in a hurry. Mind you, there's always the emergency ladder down the inside of the shaft.'

Victoria was becoming more and more despondent. 'I do wish they'd hurry,' she sighed.

'Mr Harris!' Price was calling from the doorway. 'Megan Jones and her secretary have just arrived.'

Harris turned. 'Blast!' he groaned, then sighed. 'Tell her I'll be right there.'

'Yes, sir!' Price left.

Harris brushed his usual troublesome lock of hair from his eye. 'Chief, you'd better come with me. I'm going to need some support when I talk to Megan Jones.'

'Of course, sir,' said the Chief as he followed Harris to the door.

Victoria immediately started to panic. 'But what about the Doctor and Jamie? You can't just leave them down there.'

Harris stopped at the door. 'I'm sorry,' he said, shrugging his shoulders helplessly. 'There doesn't seem to be a great deal we can do at the moment.' Then he called to Mr Oak. 'As soon as they signal, bring them up. If there's any sign of trouble, come and get me.'

'Yes, sir!' replied Mr Oak firmly, and turning to his partner said, 'You can rely on us. Isn't that so, Mr Quill?' Mr Quill nodded back confidently.

As soon as Harris and the Chief had gone, Victoria swung an uneasy glance at Mr Oak and Mr Quill. They did not exactly fill her with confidence. 'Will they be all right down there?' she asked apprehensively. 'I mean, is it safe?'

'Oh yes, Miss,' assured Mr Oak. 'Now, don't you go worrying about a thing. We'll look after them.' And again he turned to his partner. 'Won't we, Mr Quill?'

Mr Oak and Mr Quill smiled benevolently.

'Creatures? Seaweed creatures?' The Chairperson of the Board was sitting regally in a chair near the Control Cone.

She turned to her secretary, who was standing just behind her. 'What do you say to that, Perkins?'

Perkins didn't know what to say. In fact, he rarely did know what to say. He much preferred to agree with other people's comments, especially if those people happened to be his superiors. On this occasion he merely shook his head with a wry smirk.

'It's true, Miss Jones,' insisted Harris, doing his best to avoid the Chairperson's penetrating look. He hated dealing with Megan Jones. She had the reputation in the business of always getting her own way.

'You can't be serious, Mr Harris?' The Chairperson's response was cool and mocking.

'These creatures have been seen in the Refinery itself.'

Now Perkins joined in. 'By some half-witted Doctor and a couple of teenagers?'

'And by me!' snapped Harris.

'You've seen them?' asked the Chairperson.

'Yes, Miss Jones,' Harris replied firmly. 'I've seen them.'

'Mr Harris. I understand your wife . . . has had some sort of accident. This has obviously been a considerable shock to you, and . . . '

Harris resented this. 'You think I'm lying. That I was seeing things? Believe me, there are things you don't know.'

The Chairperson sat up in her seat. 'Mr Harris, I know that throughout the Southern Region, receiving stations are working on emergency supplies. What are we going to do about it?'

'At present there is nothing we can do.' Harris pointed up to the illuminated panel at the top of the Cone. 'One by one we are losing contact with the rigs out at sea.'

The Chairperson rose quickly from her seat. 'Then I suggest you send someone out there to see what's going on.'

Harris stared her out, determined not to be riled again. 'Have I your permission to call out Air Defence?'

'No, you have not. This is not a National Emergency. Use the Company helicopters.'

116

Harris was dumbfounded by such intransigence. 'Miss Jones, you don't understand the situation . . . '

'Do as I say, Mr Harris!'

Harris glared at the Chairperson, doing everything he could to control his mounting temper. But Megan Jones was in charge, and that was definitely not open to discussion. After a moment of desperate frustration, Harris turned to Price at the Control monitor. 'Get me the Chopper Hangar,' he ordered. Price duly obeyed.

Now satisfied that she was getting her own way, the Chairperson built on her authority. 'Now then, Mr Harris, I think it's time I talked with Chief Robson.'

Harris's reply was guarded. 'I'm sorry. The Chief is . . . not very well.'

'Not well? In what way?'

Harris quickly looked around his crewmen for assurance. 'Something's . . . happened to him. That's all I can tell you.'

'What?' The Chairperson was losing her patience. '*What's* happened to him.'

Harris did not reply. He tried to avoid the question by looking up at the illuminated panel on top of the Cone.

The Chairperson took two infuriated steps towards Harris and stared him straight in the face. 'Mr Harris, I'll ask you again. *What* has happened to Chief Robson?'

Harris exchanged a quick, desperate look with Price. This was one question that he just could not answer.

At the bottom of the impeller shaft, the Doctor and Jamie were straining their eyes to see in the dark. The only light available was coming from the surface of the shaft, and to Jamie that seemed like a million miles away. 'Can you see anything, Doctor?' he whispered, determined not to move an inch unless he had to.

'No, it's too dark.' The Doctor was on his hands and knees trying to look down into the Pipeline Chamber beneath the floor. 'Not a sign of van Lutyens.'

That was good enough for Jamie. 'Aye. Well no point in hanging about down here, eh?'

'Just a minute!' There was a sudden alarm in the Doctor's voice.

'What is it?'

'Listen!'

Gradually they could hear it. A faint bubbling sound beneath them.

The Doctor yelled. 'Out of here, Jamie! Quick!'

Almost as the Doctor spoke, they were completely overwhelmed by the deafening sound of the alien heartbeat. That was immediately followed by a surge of white bubbling foam, oozing into the shaft area from the pipeline chamber below. The sounds were horrifying, totally out of control. Thumping, pulsating, squealing, like a symphony of menace.

'Back to the lift, Jamie! Fast as you can.' The Doctor had to yell at the top of his voice to be heard.

There followed a mad scramble in the dark. This time, Jamie led the way, climbing back up onto the inspection ledge, hoisting the Doctor up after him. Behind them, the bubbling foam was spreading itself across the shaft area, eagerly searching out its prey.

With their backs pressed up against the metallic cylindrical wall, the Doctor and Jamie finally felt their way back to the lift. Quickly smalling down the safety rail, the Doctor yelled, 'The emergency alarm, Jamie! Press the alarm!'

'I'm pressing it!' Jamie was yelling frantically. 'It's not working.'

At surface level, the lift emergency light was flashing frenziedly. But there was no one there to answer it. No Mr Oak. No Mr Quill. No Victoria. No engineers. The place was deserted.

118

9

The Battle of the Giants

'Feed Headquarters calling Rig D. Feed Headquarters calling Rig D. Are you receiving me? Come in, please. Over!'

Watched by an anxious group including Harris, Megan Jones, Perkins, and the Chief Engineer, Price was at the Control Cone trying to re-establish visual contact with yet another rig out in the North Sea which had failed to respond to urgent messages. But the TV monitor screen serving Rig D remained defiantly blank, streaked only with distorted electrical interference.

Price tried again, his calls becoming more and more tense. 'Come in please, Rig D. Come in please! Over!'

Harris turned away from the Cone in despair. 'It's no use. There won't be a reply.'

'Don't be a fool, man!' snapped the Chairperson. 'We must keep trying. If there are men out on those rigs, there must be a reply.'

Harris swung back angrily to Megan Jones. 'If! If! If!' he growled. 'But we don't know!' He had now reached the stage where he couldn't care less if he upset authority. After all, if the North Sea Gas Network were destroyed by alien forces, there wouldn't be any jobs for anyone. 'Miss Jones,' he said, staring the Chairperson straight in the eye, 'do you understand that we have already lost contact with three of our drilling rigs?'

Now Perkins joined in. 'You say there's definitely something down in the impeller shaft blocking the flow?'

'I mean, you're absolutely sure it's not a mechanical fault?' That was the Chairperson's obvious assessment. 'You've checked the impeller?'

This time it was the Chief Engineer's turn to speak out. 'Every last nut and bolt has been checked!' His voice was firm and confident. 'Whatever it is that's blocking the flow has nothing to do with mechanical failure. The problem is out of our control, right there, down in that shaft!'

The Chairperson swung a look of disbelief at the Chief Engineer. Then she slowly turned, to see the groups of anxious faces all around the Communications Hall, watching and waiting for her response.

For the first time the Chairperson was beginning to take the situation seriously.

The impeller shaft was under siege. Not only was the thumping heartbeat sound swelling to an unbearable pitch, but the smell of toxic gas fumes was beginning to seep into the thin air.

The Doctor and Jamie were clutching their ears in agony. They were trapped inside the lift which stubbornly refused to ascend, leaving the bubbling white foam easy access to them as it surged over the top of the inspection ledge just a short distance from the lift itself.

Jamie had to shout to be heard. 'Why don't they operate the lift!'

'I don't know!' yelled the Doctor. 'But we can't wait much longer!'

Jamie tried calling out as loud as he could. 'Victoria! Hey! All of you up there – help!' His voice only seemed to provoke the alien sounds into an even greater frenzy.

'It's no good, Jamie!' yelled the Doctor. 'They can't hear us!'

Jamie was suddenly chilled with terror. 'Doctor – look!'

His eyes were rivetted towards something just beneath them in the shaft area. Through the dim pool of light that was beaming down from the surface, they could just see the silhouette of a huge shapeless form rising up from the foam. It was the Weed Creature, writhing, wriggling, squealing, its throbbing tendrils stretching out in every direction.

'Let's get out of here, Jamie – quick!' The Doctor raised the safety rail, and stepped out of the lift. But Jamie didn't follow him. His eyes were transfixed on the towering, ghostly apparition in the foam. He was too numb to move. 'Jamie!' The Doctor yelled at the top of his voice, and shook Jamie hard by the shoulders.

Jamie shivered, as though waking from a nightmare. 'Doctor! W-what is it?'

The Doctor grabbed hold of him, and dragged him out of the lift. 'It's all right, Jamie! Just follow me – and stay awake!'

The Doctor made straight for the steel emergency ladder that ran up the side of the wall to the surface. 'Keep right behind me!' he yelled to Jamie. 'And whatever you do, don't lose your concentration!'

Jamie did as he was told, and followed the Doctor up the ladder. As soon as they moved, the Weed Creature squealed and hissed aloud in anger. Then its colony of small seaweed clumps began popping to the surface of the foam.

'Doctor!' The toxic gas fumes were beginning to affect Jamie, and he was coughing and spluttering, on the verge of a sneezing fit.

'Up the ladder, Jamie! Keep climbing!'

'Doctor!'

The first of the weed tendrils was beginning to wind itself around the base of the ladder.

Jamie let out a loud sneeze. 'Doctor! I can't . . . I can't . . . '
The weed tendril was just two steps beneath his feet.

The Doctor shouted back with all the strength at his command. 'Keep climbing, Jamie! Don't look down!'

Along the Compound corridor leading from the Impeller Area, one of the blue-painted doors was marked *PIPELINE ROOM. AUTHORISED PERSONNEL ONLY*. The door opened. Mr Oak came out first, then Mr Quill. Mr Oak locked the door behind him, put the key into his pocket, then exchanged a sly smile with Mr Quill.

Like a silent movie comedy double-act, the two men moved off side by side, and disappeared down the corridor . . .

In the Impeller Area, the lift emergency light was still flashing wildly. But there was no one around to answer it.

After a moment, a loud sneeze from Jamie was heard echoing down the shaft.

'Hold on, Jamie! We're nearly there!' The Doctor's head popped up over the edge of the shaft. Gasping for breath, he quickly climbed off the emergency ladder, then turned back to help Jamie. Are you all right?'

'Aye, I think so. What a climb!' Jamie's eyes were sore from the gas fumes, and he could hardly breathe. But he managed to jump down from the shaft ledge without falling.

The Doctor peered back down the shaft. 'We're lucky to get out alive. The weed must be filling the entire shaft!'

'Aye, and it was moving fast too!' The sooner we get out of this place, the better!' Jamie started to move towards the door, then stopped to look around. 'Hey, wait a minute. Where's Victoria!'

The Doctor was feeling decidedly apprehensive and uneasy. 'No wonder our signal was ignored,' he said suspiciously. 'There's nobody here.' He turned to the lift controls, and turned off the flashing emergency light.

Jamie was more puzzled than ever. 'But Victoria would never have left us.'

'You're right, Jamie,' said the Doctor grimly. 'Not unless somebody persuaded her to!'

Jamie looked up sharply at the Doctor. The thought that Victoria might be in danger filled him with horror. His response was immediate and determined: 'We've got to find her!'

The Communications Hall was now on full alert. Not only was the impeller at a standstill, but the gas flow to the South of England was completely cut off. Even more serious was the fact that both audio and visual contact between the Refinery and its rigs had broken down. And now came the news that Megan Jones found absolutely shattering to even contemplate. 'Foam and weed on all the rigs?' said the Chairperson incredulously. 'Mr Harris, are you sure you've heard right?'

Harris was ashen-faced. 'According to the helicopter pilot, there is no sign of life at all on any one of the rigs.'

There was a deathly silence throughout the Hall. All that could be heard was the intermittent flickering of lights at the Control Cone.

'I don't believe it. I just – don't believe it!' The Chairperson could hardly bring herself to speak. She raised herself out of her chair, and turned to look up at the illuminated panel on top of the Cone. 'All this – it's so fantastic!' Then, turning back to Harris she asked helplessly, 'What can we do?'

For once in his life, Harris was decisive in his reply. 'Our main priority is to save the lives of any of the crew who may still be alive..

'What do you suggest?'

'Give me permission to evacuate them. Then blow every one of the rigs to pieces – right out of the sea!'

'*What*!' The Chairperson's secretary looked as though he was about to have a fit. 'You'rre out of your mind, Harris! Have you any idea how much those rigs cost to install?' He then pleaded directly with the Chairperson. 'Miss Jones, you can't agree to such a thing. Euro-Gas is of vital economic importance to the Government, to the country. The Minister would never forgive us if we . . . '

'To hell with the Minister!' bawled Harris. 'The lives of our crews are more important than any one of those rigs!'

Perkins was practically purple in the face with indignation. 'Our duty,' he spluttered pompously, 'is to the British electorate!'

'Shut up, Perkins!' snapped the Chairperson. Perkins stared at her in disbelief. He felt like a balloon that had been pricked with a pin. The Chairperson quickly turned to Harris. In an extraordinary way, being put on the defensive made her look more attractive. 'Mr Harris,' she said calmly, 'You ask me to destroy years of hard work, skill, and Government money . . . '

Harris felt no guilt at interrupting her. 'Miss Jones, I am asking you to destroy this evil that's in the sea. Destroy it – before it's too late. I implore you – bomb the rigs – now!'

'No! Never!' A voice was booming out from the other side of the Hall. Everyone turned to look. The shadow of a man was standing in the doorway of the Compound exit. It was Robson.

'Mr Robson!' The Chairperson was visibly shaken as she caught her first glimpse of Robson. He came rushing across the Hall towards her, his appearance a shock to everyone. Heavy-eyed, tired, drawn, and unshaven, the Controller seemed to be on the very brink of a nervous breakdown.

'Leave the rigs alone!' Robson's demand was directed as much to Harris and everyone in the Hall as to the Chairperson herself. 'They're mine I tell you – mine!'

The Chairperson took a nervous step backwards. She was staring at Robson in wide-eyed amazement. Was this the man to whom she had entrusted so much power – ? The man whose career she herself had promoted? 'Robson . . . ' she asked falteringly, 'what is it? What's wrong?'

Robson turned his back on her, and launched into a wild discourse to everyone in the Hall who was staring at him. As he spoke, there was a look of madness in his eyes. 'Can't you see it?' he yelled, his voice now back to its old harsh, loud tone. 'Can't you see they're all against me? Those rigs – they're mine! Mine! I built them with my own sweat and blood. They're my life! They want to destroy everything because they know it'll destroy me! But I won't let . . . we won't allow . . . we . . . ' His voice gradually faltered. He seemed puzzled and uncertain.

'*We*, Robson?' asked the Chairperson. 'Who are you referring to?'

Robson turned suddenly to look at her. It was as though he was only just aware that there was someone else in the Hall. 'What?' he murmured. 'My . . . I . . . I don't know . . . ' He began to stagger, then clutched his hand to his forehead as if in pain.

'Mr Robson!' The Chief Engineer rushed forward to help Robson. Harris and two other engineers did likewise.

'Is he all right?' asked the Chairperson.

Robson suddenly sprang to life again, and shrugged off the help he was being given. 'Of course I'm all right . . . ' Everyone became aware of the change in his voice. It had resumed its soft, almost inaudible tone. For a brief moment he stood quite still, looking around him from face to face in disorientated bewilderment. 'I'm sorry,' he mumbled breathlessly, 'I don't know what I . . . ' Without another word, he broke free from the group around him, and rushed out of the Hall. Everyone watched him go in shocked disbelief.

'Mr Robson!' called the Chairperson.

Harris said, 'Let him go. The strain must have affected his mind.'

'It's not the strain, I can assure you.' This time it was the Doctor's voice. He was approaching from the Impeller Area.

The Chairperson glared at the stranger. 'And who the devil are you?'

Harris turned with a start. 'Doctor! I'd almost forgotten. What about van Lutyens? Did you find him?'

Even before Harris had finished asking the question, the Doctor was shaking his head sadly. This was yet another

shock which Harris found hard to accept. He swallowed hard
and asked, 'Have you any idea what happened?'

'Unfortunately, yes, I have. Jamie and I very nearly
suffered the same fate. The whole of the bottom of that shaft
is filled with weed and foam.'

There was a shock wave of horror throughout the Hall.

'What's this all about?' asked the Chairperson impatiently. 'What's happened to Mr van Lutyens?'

The Doctor shrugged his shoulders.

'And what about Mr Robson?'

The Doctor hesitated before answering. 'Mr Robson, I
fear,' he said gravely, 'is being controlled by some kind of
mental force which emanates from this weed.'

Each face around the hall showed the same expression:
fear and horror.

After a moment's stunned silence, the Chairperson spoke.
'This is preposterous! You expect me to believe such an
incredible suggestion?'

Harris brushed the usual lock of hair from his eye. 'That's
what we've said so far about everything the Doctor has told
us. But each time he's been proved right.' He turned
pointedly to the Chairperson. 'I think it's about time we
started believing him.'

The Chairperson hesitated, uncertain what to do. Then
she sat down in her chair again, took a deep breath, and said,
'Very well. The least I can do is to listen.'

'Victoria! Victoria, where are you?'

Jamie's frantic calls echoed throughout the Refinery. He
was desperate to find Victoria before any harm came to her.
Jamie knew that something terrible must have happened to
her, for nothing in the world would have persuaded Victoria
to abandon the Doctor and himself at a time when their lives
were at risk. Time and time again he kept asking himself
how Victoria could have disappeared from the impeller area
without anyone knowing.

'Victoria!' he called again. 'Can you hear me . . . ?'

Jamie eventually found himself in a dimly lit corridor which led to the Impeller Area at the far end. It wasn't surprising that he missed seeing the corridor when he first started searching for Victoria, for most of the rooms and corridors in the Refinery looked identical.

Half-way down the corridor he stopped at a blue-painted door which was marked, *PIPELINE ROOM. AUTHORISED PERSONNEL ONLY*. He banged on the door and called, 'Victoria! Are you in there?' No reply. He tried the door handle. Locked. There was a small glass panel in the door. He peered through. He gasped with horror at what he could see inside.

'Victoria!'

Inside the pipeline room, Victoria was lying spread-eagled on the steps of the platform in front of the transparent section of the pipeline. She looked as though she was dead.

Jamie went beserk, tried to break open the door by throwing himself against it. The door wouldn't budge. He quickly looked around to see what he could use to force it open. But the corridor was quite bare except for a pile of metal boxes. Then he noticed a ventilator grille just above the door. Dragging some of the metal boxes over to the door to make a platform, he clambered up on to them and started to heave at the grille.

In the Communications Hall, everyone was standing around in awed silence, listening to the Doctor. The Chairperson clearly found the Doctor's theories almost too wildly incredible to believe. Tapping her fingers unconsciously on the side of her chair she asked, 'You're trying to tell me that this seaweed – or whatever it is – is a living organism, capable of exercising some sort of telepathic control over human life?'

The Doctor was firm in his reply: 'Yes!'

'But seaweed is a vegetable matter. Everybody knows that.'

The Doctor started to pace up and down. 'This is a

struggle for power, Miss Jones – matter over mind. I'm convinced that these people – Mrs Harris, Chief Robson, and Mr van Lutyens – have all been overcome by this struggle.' He stopped, and turned. 'And goodness knows how many more.'

Harris was completely bewildered. 'But where does the weed get this super-intelligence from, Doctor?'

'From the human brain. The weed is a parasite.'

The full implication of what the Doctor was saying suddenly showed in Harris's tense reaction. 'You mean . . . these creatures have taken over . . . human beings?'

The Doctor shook his head gravely. 'I don't know. But they're certainly instruments of the weed colony.'

Everyone suddenly turned with a dramatic start as a red flashing light began to buzz on the illuminated panel above the Cone.

Price called urgently from his seat at the Cone. 'Mr Harris! Control Rig!'

Harris rushed to the Cone, where the face of Chief Baxter at the Control Rig immediately appeared on the main television monitor screen. 'Chief!' he yelled. 'Where the hell have you been? We've been trying to contact you for the past five hours!'

Baxter was in a terrified state, almost hysterical. As he spoke, he was continually looking all around him. 'Mr Harris!' he spluttered, his face pouring with sweat. 'For God's sake! They're . . . all around us!'

Harris shared a stunned glance with the Chairperson. 'What are you talking about, Chief? What's going on out there?' The Hall was suddenly shattered by the piercing sound of crewmen screaming on the monitor, somewhere near the Chief.

Baxter struggled to speak, but the picture was beginning to vibrate. 'Those things . . . the place is alive with them . . . they're everywhere . . . we can't hold on – ' He was interrupted by even more terrifying screams, which chilled the blood of everyone watching the monitor screen. Baxter stared straight into the camera that was gradually going out of focus. He was desperate. 'Get us out of here! Somebody get us out of – '

Everyone in the Hall watched the monitor screen in helpless shock and horror. Chief Baxter was screaming out hysterically as a sudden upsurge of white bubbling foam started to engulf him.

'Baxter!' Harris shouted at the monitor screen. 'Baxter! Can you hear me?'

Within seconds it was all over. The picture on the screen disappeared, and was replaced by distorted lines and electrical interference.

'Feed Headquarters calling Control Rig. Feed Headquarters calling Control Rig. Are you receiving me please? Over!' Price was operating every switch available to regain contact with Baxter. He called again. 'Control Rig. Come in please. Over!'

The monitor screen remained defiantly unresponsive.

Price turned from the Cone, thoroughly defeated. 'We've lost contact.'

There was a hushed, stunned silence throughout the Hall. The Chairperson cupped her face in her hands.

The metal ventilator grille above the pipeline room door crashed to the floor with a loud clang. Within a few moments, Jamie had eased himself through the grille opening, falling with a thud to the floor on the other side.

He quickly picked himself up, and rushed across to where Victoria was lying spread-eagled in front of the transparent section of the pipeline tube. He stooped down in a desperate effort to revive her. 'Victoria!' he called anxiously. 'Victoria, can you hear me?'

There was no response from Victoria. Her face and body remained quite motionless.

Thinking that Victoria was dead, Jamie became very distressed. Memories instantly flooded through his mind. Memories of all the good times he'd had with Victoria, of the many adventures they had shared with the Doctor. It was a pathetic, endearing sight to see the sturdy Highland lad from eighteenth-century Scotland kneeling beside the lifeless body of the young Victorian girl who had been his close companion for so long. Did it really have to end like this, he wondered, after all they had been through together? Jamie drew closer to Victoria. He talked gently to her, rubbed her hand, and stroked her forehead. It was his own simple way of trying to inject life back into her. 'Oh Victoria,' he whispered, his voice cracking with emotion, 'you can't be . . . you just can't be . . . '

What he hadn't noticed was that Victoria's eyes were flickering half-open.

Jamie swallowed hard. He felt there was a lump in his throat the size of an apple. 'If anything's happened to you, I . . . I don't know what I'd do . . . '

'Why, Jamie, I didn't know you cared . . . '

Jamie sat back with a start. 'Victoria Waterfield!' He quickly brushed the suggestion of a tear from his eye. 'You tricked me! That's not fair!'

Victoria sat up, still a little dazed. 'I did not! I was unconscious!'

'What are you doing here?' scolded Jamie. 'What happened?'

Victoria cleared her throat, which felt very dry. 'It was those two engineers.'

'What engineers?'

'You know who I mean.' Victoria used her hands to mime a description of Mr Oak and Mr Quill. 'The short man and . . . the tall, thin one.'

Jamie suddenly recalled the identical white jackets and caps. 'Oh yes. That weird pair that sent us down in the lift.'

'I don't remember. I just passed out.'

'Aye, well just wait 'til I get my hands on them! It must have been their fault that the Doctor and me very nearly got . . . well, never mind that now. At least no harm's come to you.'

Victoria was now sitting up, resting her chin on her hands. She looked thoroughly depressed. 'Oh Jamie,' she sighed, 'why are we always getting into trouble like this? Everywhere we go it's always the same.'

Jamie looked concerned. 'How d'you mean?'

'I don't know,' said Victoria, staring aimlessly at the floor. 'I'm just fed up, that's all. I'm tired of one crisis on top of another. I just want . . . well, some peace and quiet.'

Jamie's face crumpled. He felt quite hurt. 'But aren't you happy with the Doctor and me?'

'Yes, but . . . oh, never mind. I suppose I'm just . . . ' Victoria stopped speaking abruptly, and looked up with a start.

'What's the matter?'

'Listen!' Victoria looked up towards the ceiling, then all around.

Jamie's head was rigid, but his eyes were darting all over the room. 'What is it?'

The girl's voice became a strangulated whisper. 'Listen! Can't you hear it?'

Both of them sat absolutely still, hardly daring to move a muscle. It was the faint approach of the heartbeat sound. This time it came as a metallic echo.

'Where's it coming from?' whispered Jamie tensely.

'Even as he spoke, the alien sound exploded into a deafening roar.

Jamie and Victoria sprang to their feet. 'Look!' yelled Jamie. Both turned, and squirmed in horror at what they saw behind them.

The transparent section of the huge pipeline tube was crawling with clumps of pulsating seaweed, all wriggling in a mass of oozing white foam.

In the Control Hall, the Doctor was pointing up to the illuminated panel at the top of the Cone. The indicator light was no longer operating for the Control Rig, and only three rig lights remained: rigs B, E, and F.

'Now that the Control Rig has gone,' said the Doctor urgently, 'that leave us with just one conclusion.' He turned, to direct his assessment straight to the Chairperson and Harris. 'The Weed is trying to take over all the rigs, forming itself into a vast colony.'

The Chairperson frowned. 'With what objective?' she asked.

'The saturation of the British Isles and in time, perhaps the entire planet.'

Perkins spoke. For the first time, sneering disbelief was giving way to genuine fear. 'Is such a thing possible?' he asked.

'It is,' replied the Doctor with complete conviction. 'Unless we can find the nerve centre of the colony and destroy it.'

The Chairperson exchanged a puzzled glance with Harris. 'How could we possibly do that?' she said. 'It may be anywhere out in the North Sea.'

'Precisely,' said the Doctor, sounding a note of warning. 'That's the problem.'

'Doctor!'

Everyone in the Hall turned with a start to see Jamie and Victoria calling from the door of the Impeller Area.

'The pipeline!' yelled Jamie.

'Please hurry!' Victoria was practically screeching.

By the time the Doctor and everyone had reached the pipeline room, the transparent section of the pipeline tube was jammed solid with the oozing mass of seaweed clumps and white bubbling foam.

For a few moments, the group just stared in silent horror at the awesome sight before them. The thumping heartbeat sound was frenetic, and the Chairperson had to shout to be heard. 'In heaven's name – what *is* that?' she spluttered from a safe distance near the door.

'The advance guard.' The Doctor moved into the room, his eyes transfixed on the squirming mass of seaweed tendrils inside the pipeline tube.

'I don't understand,' shouted the Chairperson. 'What's happening?'

'The first part of the invasion . . . ' The Doctor moved a few steps closer towards the pipeline tube.

'No, Doctor!' Victoria was yelling from the door. 'Don't go any nearer!'

On hearing Victoria's voice, the Doctor stopped dead. 'It's begun!' he said, addressing the warning more to himself than to the other. He was staring hard at the pipeline tube. 'The battle of the giants!'

Inside the pipeline tube, the thumping heartbeat sound was pounding louder and louder, the white foam was bubbling, and the seaweed clumps were squealing. And in the middle of it all, the weed tendrils groped uncontrollably at the transparent walls. They were determined to find a way out . . .

10

The Spy Within

The Communications Hall was like a mausoleum. There were no flashing lights on the illuminated panel above the Control Cone, and every one of the television monitor screens was blank. Amongst the Communications crew there was a mixture of apathy and fear, and after the long hours of endless duty, total exhaustion. Everyone was in a state of high tension, watching and waiting for the weed's next move.

At the Control Cone, Price was relentlessly trying to re-establish contact with the rigs out at sea. Over and over again his weary voice could be heard echoing throughout the Hall, calling out to the lifeless two-way monitor screens.

'Feed Headquarters calling Rig F. Feed Headquarters calling Rig F. Are you receiving me? Come in please. Over!'

Anxious moments whilst everyone waited for a response. But the central monitor screen remained stubbornly silent.

Chairperson Megan Jones hurried into the Hall from the Impeller Area. Harris, Perkins, the Doctor, Jamie, and Victoria were with her.

'Mr Harris sir!' Price called immediately from the Cone. 'I can't raise any of the rigs.'

Harris went quickly to the Cone. 'None of them?'

'Not one, sir. I'll try again.' He turned back to the monitors again, and repeated his emergency calls. 'Feed Headquarters calling Rig B. Feed Headquarters calling Rig B. Are you receiving me? Come in please. Over!'

Once again, the same dead reaction from both monitor and illuminated panel. Price turned from the Cone to give Harris a sad shake of the head.

'Keep trying man!' insisted Miss Jones in desperation. Reluctantly, Price turned back to continue repeating his video calls to the rigs.

'You're wasting your time, Miss Jones,' said the Doctor. 'By now those rigs will be part of the weed colony.'

'I don't care about the rigs,' bawled Harris. 'What's happened to the men out there?'

All the Doctor could do was to shake his head slowly, despondently.

Harris's frustration suddenly exploded. 'Then we've got to destroy the rigs! Every one of them!'

'No!' yelled the Chairperson defiantly. 'Never!'

The Doctor agreed. 'No, Mr Harris. We daren't do that.'

'Why not?'

'Because it would spread this menace over a wide area and make it almost impossible to attack.'

'Well, what are we supposed to do?' snapped Harris. 'Just sit here and wait to be destroyed?'

'More important, Mr Harris,' said the Doctor, trying to calm Harris's high state of tension, 'is to know what the *Weed* is going to do.'

There was a moment's pause, then the Chairperson asked, 'What *can* it do?'

'Let's think,' suggested the Doctor. He started pacing up and down, quickly trying to calculate the true extent of the seaweed menace. 'Now . . . I suppose the weed was first drawn up through the drilling rigs?'

'No,' said Harris. 'Anything that comes up through those

135

bores would be cleared by the engineers at source. Otherwise it would block the pumps.'

'Precisely!' The Doctor stopped pacing, and turned back to Harris. 'And the engineers who cleared it would probably have come into physical contact with it. In other words, they'd have touched it in some way or another?'

'Yes . . . I see what you mean.' Harris was beginning to understand what the Doctor was getting at. 'Those engineers would have been the first to have come under the direct control of the weed.'

The Doctor's mind was now racing. 'Since then, this attack – and it is an attack – has followed a pattern.'

The Chairperson asked, 'How d'you mean?'

'I mean, Miss Jones, that the top priority people in the Euro-Gas network have been affected first.'

'If your theory is correct,' estimated the Chairperson, 'this weed now controls two vital people who know the entire layout and structure of the Refinery compound.'

The Doctor scratched the back of his head, and sighed. 'Unfortunately, that is true.'

After thinking carefully for a brief moment, the Chairperson turned quickly to Harris and said urgently, 'Robson was here not so very long ago. We must find him and prevent the weed from using him – for his own sake as well as ours!'

Harris agreed and went straight to Price at the Control Cone. 'Get Security to search the entire Compound. I want Mr Robson found and put under armed guard in his cabin.'

Price nodded, and immediately put a call through to Security.

Harris returned to the Doctor. 'One thing doesn't fit in with your theory,' he said, trying to work things out. 'The fact that your friend Victoria was attacked in the Oxygen Room. She has absolutely nothing whatever to do with the personnel here.'

'Yes. That's one thing that's been puzzling me.' The Doctor considered this carefully for a moment, then continued. 'Victoria disturbed someone who was attempting to interfere with the oxygen supply . . . '

'Yes. Someone wearing a gas mask.'

The Doctor reacted sharply. 'Of course! Now if that person was under the control of the weed then he was wearing a gas mask for one reason only!'

'Because to him, pure oxygen would be toxic!'

The Doctor thumped his fist into his hand excitedly. 'Exactly!'

Amongst a group of engineers listening nearby were Mr Oak and Mr Quill, who exchanged a pointed glance with each other. Without saying a word, both slipped out of the Hall unnoticed.

Now it was Harris's turn to become excited. The Doctor had given him the first glimmer of hope. 'Oxygen! That's the key to it all! We can use it as a weapon against the weed.'

The Doctor held up his hands to advise caution. 'At the moment, it's only a theory . . . '

For the first time, the Chairperson directed a smile of confidence towards the Doctor. 'As Mr Harris said before, you've been right so far, there's no reason why you shouldn't be now.'

'How nice to be trusted!' replied the Doctor, beaming. 'I only hope I'm right!'

The Chairperson's smile quickly faded.

Mr Oak and Mr Quill waddled down the corridor from the Communications Hall. They stopped briefly at the door marked, *OXYGEN STORE ROOM*, quickly checked the corridor to make sure no-one could see them, then entered.

The Oxygen Room was in darkness; Mr Oak and Mr Quill preferred it that way. First they put on their white gloves, then their gas masks, which they carried across their shoulders. After nodding to each other, they made their way to the rows of oxygen cylinders stacked on the shelves. One by one they turned on the release taps.

Two sinister white-clad figures moved around in the dark. The room was filled with the sound of hissing gas . . .

Jamie and Victoria were watching the Doctor, who was deep in thought. They had seen him like this so many times before, eyes transfixed to the ground, like a general trying to work out the enemy's next move.

On the other side of the Communications Hall, Harris was with Megan Jones and Perkins in the office area. All three were slouched wearily in chairs, sipping black coffee from thick Company mugs. Not a word was spoken between them. Secretly, each of them were hoping that the Doctor would come up with some miracle solution that would save them all from disaster.

'Mr Harris sir!' All three turned. Price was calling from the Control Cone. 'They've found Mr Robson!'

Harris rose immediately and rushed across. 'Where is he?'

'In his cabin, sir. Apparently he was just lying on his bunk. There's a guard outside his door.'

'Good! Tell Security to keep him there. I'm on my way over right now!'

'I want to see him, Harris,' called the Chairperson, as she hurried across from the office with Perkins.

'I strongly advise against it, Miss Jones,' warned Harris. 'Mr Robson is a very ill man.'

The Chairperson had that stubborn look in her eyes again. 'I *want* to see him.'

'But you've seen him already. It's obvious he's in no fit state to help us in any way.'

'Let me be the judge of that, Harris. Mr Robson and I are old friends. If he knows something, I'm the person he'll confide in.'

Harris sighed. He knew better than to argue with the woman. She always used seniority rather than reason to get her own way. 'Very well, Miss Jones. But I warn you, Mr Robson is in an unpredictable state at the moment. He could be violent.'

The Chairperson didn't bother to listen to Harris. She was already on her way out of the Hall. Harris and Perkins followed her obediently.

'But why not ask the Minister to request some assistance from the National Defences?' Perkins suggested, as he trailed behind the Chairperson along the main Compound corridor.

'Don't talk rot, man!' snapped the lady dismissively. 'What exactly do you suppose the armed forces could do?'

'Well . . . attack this . . . this weed stuff, or whatever it is.'

'How? If we attack the rigs, what about the men out there?'

'But we don't know there are any men left on the rigs?'

The Chairperson stopped abruptly and turned on Perkins. He was getting on her nerves. 'Equally, we don't know that they aren't still there! They may be prisoners - anything! And even if we do blow the rigs out of the sea, there's no guarantee that will be the end of this - this nightmare. For all we know, it could even spread the menace, just like that Doctor fellow suggested.'

Perkins twitched uneasily, utterly deafeated.

Harris quickly interrupted them. 'This way please, Miss Jones.'

The Chairperson glared contemptuously at Perkins, then followed Harris into an adjoining corridor.

An armed Security Guard was on duty outside Robson's cabin. As Harris, the Chairperson, and Perkins approached, he straightened up a little and tried to look efficient.

Harris was worried. 'Look, Miss Jones. I think it would be far safer if you let me or Mr Perkins come in with you.'

The Chairperson waved her hand dismissively. 'Stop fussing, man! I shall be perfectly all right.'

Harris hesitated, still uncertain. Then he nodded to the Guard, who unlocked the door. Without another word, the Chairperson entered Robson's cabin.

Robson was lying on his bunk, eyes staring aimlessly at

the ceiling. His face was white, gaunt, and lined, and his hair was even more streaked with white than when Harris had first noticed it on the beach.

The Chairperson came in, and closed the door behind her. She turned to look at Robson, but hesitated before going across to him. 'Robson,' she called quietly. No reply. She tried again. 'Robson.' Still no reply, not even a flicker of recognition. Slowly, cautiously, she moved towards the bunk and looked down at Robson. She was shocked by his appearance.

'John,' she called in a gentle whisper. 'John, can you hear me?'

After a moment's pause, Robson slowly turned his head towards her. There was a faint glimmer of recognition in his eyes. His face was streaked with perspiration, and it was obvious that he was under considerable mental strain.

'It's all right, John. It's me – Megan. Megan Jones.'

Robson just stared aimlessly at her. There was no sign of life in his eyes.

'We want to try and help you.'

'Help . . . ?' Robson struggled to speak. But his voice was bewildered, barely audible.

Megan drew closer. 'Tell me what happened, John . . . '

Robson shook his head.

'Try, John! We can't help you unless you try!'

There was panic in Robson's eyes. And desperation. 'Nobody . . . nobody can help . . . '

'We *can* help you, John, but only if you let us. Whatever it is that's affecting you, you've got to fight it!'

'No!' Robson suddenly sat bolt upright. His eyes began to dart frantically around the room in every direction.

Megan grabbed him firmly by the shoulders. She tried to be the Chairperson with him again, to bring him back to reality. 'Now listen to me, Robson!' she snapped, 'just remember that I am the one who put you in charge of this Refinery, and I can just as easily send you right back to the rigs! Do you want that, Robson? Do you?' She watched him in horrified disbelief as he started to breathe quickly and heavily. But her only feeble response was to shake him by his shoulders and bawl, 'Pull yourself together man!'

Robson's frantic breathing stopped suddenly, and his eyes glazed over. Megan felt as though she was holding on to a marble statue. 'What is it, John?' she asked tensely. 'Tell me!'

It seemed like hours before Robson's reply. He slowly turned and stared at her, his mind battling with the telepathic control of the weed. 'Meg-an . . . ' His mouth was struggling to form the words. 'I . . . I . . . ' He stopped dead. The sound was beginning to take over. The thumping, heartbeat sound, pulverising his mind into submission. He clutched his ears in agony and yelled out, '*Help me*!'

Megan held on to his shoulders and gradually eased him back onto the pillow. 'Easy now, John . . . easy . . . '

Robson's agonising shout brought Harris bursting into the room. 'Miss Jones! Are you all right?'

Megan didn't reply. She was trying to comfort Robson, who was quiet now, his eyes once again staring aimlessly. 'Robson,' she whispered gently. 'John, can you hear me?'

Robson remained absolutely still. There was not even a flicker from him now, no response or sign of recognition. Megan watched him for a moment or so, then stood up. She turned, and shook her head in despair at Harris and Perkins, who were standing in the doorway. 'It's as if he were in a trance or something – hypnotised. I thought for a moment he was going to be rational, but . . . '

Harris said, 'We'd better let him rest.'

Megan nodded in agreement, and after taking a last worried look back to Robson in his bunk, she returned to the corridor with Harris and Perkins.

Harris closed the cabin door, and the Security Guard moved back into position.

Megan was clearly distressed. 'Isn't there anything we can do for him, Harris?'

Harris shook his head. 'The Doctor couldn't help my

wife. We're up against something we know nothing about.'

Megan turned to look at him, and straightened up. She was the Chairperson again. There was a new surge of determination in her. 'Then the only thing that will help any of us – as far as I can see – is to destroy that weed.' Without saying another word, she marched off down the corridor in the direction of the Control Hall.

Harris and Perkins exchanged a brief look of surprise, then followed her.

In the Control Hall, Jamie and Victoria were watching the Doctor, who was deep in thought, sitting on the steps leading up to the pipeline inspection area. Every so often he would mumble something under his breath, a sure sign that he was trying to work out some kind of logical plan.

'He's really worried now,' said Jamie anxiously. 'He's beginning to give me the willies!'

Victoria crossed her arms and sighed despondently. 'Yes. I just wish we could go back to the TARDIS and get away from all this trouble.'

'Och, we couldna' do that! The Doctor would never leave all these people, not when they're facing up to so much danger . . .'

'Oh I know, I know!' snapped Victoria irritably.

Jamie turned to look at her, aware that she was in a bad mood again. 'You don't have to bite my head off, y'know!'

Victoria threw him a tetchy look without replying.

'The Doctor's got enough trouble on his hands trying to find out what's going on round here. You know, it's odd. He says there definitely *is* an obvious answer to this weed stuff.'

'Answer? What d'you mean?'

'You know, some way of fighting it.'

'It can't be that obvious,' said Victoria dismissively, 'otherwise he'd have thought of it!'

The Chairperson entered the Hall with Harris and Perkins. They went straight to the Doctor.

'Well, Doctor, have you thought of any means by which

142

we can attack this . . . weed?' The Chairperson had a way of sounding aggressive without actually being so.

The Doctor looked up from his reverie. 'Hmm? Oh . . . no, Miss Jones. Not yet, I'm afraid.'

'What about the weed? What do you think it will do next?'

The Doctor raised himself up from the step he was sitting on. 'I think it has little alternative but to attack us . . . right here!'

Once again everyone in the Hall turned to look at the Doctor.

'Here?' spluttered Harris. 'In the Refinery?'

'Yes!' The Doctor was quite firm in his reply.

'But what could make you think such a thing?' This was the first time Perkins had contributed anything to the discussion.

The Doctor put his hands behind his back and looked around the vast Control Hall. 'This Refinery is the pivot of the gas distribution network. If the weed is to survive and expand, it has to gain control right here! Our only hope is to find the nerve-centre of the weed colony – and destroy it.'

Everyone in the Hall exchanged glances with each other in stunned silence. Surprisingly, it was Perkins who asked the crucial question. 'But where is this nerve centre?'

'We don't know.' The Doctor was more grave-faced than either Jamie or Victoria could remember. 'That's just *one* of the problems.'

'And we're not sure yet quite how to destroy it, are we?' Harris brushed his usual troublesome lock of hair from his eye.

'No,' said the Doctor falteringly, 'but . . . there's something at the back of my mind which . . . '

'What about the oxygen?' suggested Harris.

The Doctor looked up sharply. 'The oxygen? Yes. It's a possibility.'

'Right!' said the Chairperson, quick to assert her authority. Turning to Harris she bawled, 'Put the Oxygen Supply Room under guard – immediately!'

Robson was lying on his bunk where Megan Jones had left him. For once, his eyes were closed, and he was fast asleep.

Suddenly, his eyes sprang open and immediately focussed on the ventilator grille in the ceiling directly above his head. For several moments he kept absolutely still. Either he wouldn't move, or he couldn't.

To Robson, the grille appeared as a vast dark cavern. Something was there looking down at him, watching, waiting . . .

The thumping heartbeat sound was very faint. But as it grew in intensity, the expression on Robson's face was clear and decisive. He was receiving instructions.

In the corridor outside Robson's cabin, the armed guard, tired from long hours on duty, drooped with fatigue. Behind him, Robson's glazed, staring eyes watched him through the perspex panel in the door.

The door slowly opened, and in one swift moment, Robson's hand slammed over the guard's mouth. The hand was covered with a hair-like weed formation. The guard struggled, but Robson suddenly opened his mouth wide to emit a loud, hissing lethal gas. The guard's eyes gradually glazed over, and he slumped to the ground unconscious.

Robson stood quite motionless for a moment, staring down at the guard's lifeless body. Gradually the thumping heartbeat sound began to enter the dark caverns of his brain. His eyes flicked up sharply. He was listening, taking instructions again. In a moment, he was gone.

At the Control Cone, Harris was reacting with incredulity at the news Price had just passed to him. 'The whole of the Oxygen Store?'

'I'm afraid so, sir,' replied Price. 'There are no reserves left at all.'

Harris took a deep breath and turned to the Doctor. 'They seem to be one step ahead of us all the time.'

144

'Exactly as I thought,' said the Doctor, turning to look with deep suspicion at the group gathered around the Cone. 'Robson is not the only one here to be controlled by the weed colony.'

The Chairperson fumbled nervously with the string of pearls hanging around her neck. 'You mean, there's some kind of a spy amongst us?'

'Yes.' The Doctor was adamant. 'And maybe more than one of them.'

There was a tense pause. Nobody hardly dared to breathe.

Harris spluttered, 'But . . . how do we find out who they are?'

The Doctor shrugged his shoulders. 'That's the difficulty.'

Everyone in the Hall was now casting an uneasy glance at the person standing next to them. Megan Jones, the Doctor, Perkins, Harris, Jamie, the Chief Engineer, Victoria, Price, the Communications crewmen – all of them studied each other with the deepest suspicion. Victoria in particular did a double-take. She was alarmed to catch a glimpse of Mr Oak and Mr Quill hiding amongst a group of engineers on the other side of the Hall.

'We must have a personnel check,' called Harris urgently. 'Everybody in the Compound!'

Victoria quickly turned to Jamie to draw his attention to Mr Oak and Mr Quill. But by the time Jamie looked up, the indefatigable duo had gone.

Mr Oak and Mr Quill hurried down the corridor from the Control Hall. They couldn't run because they didn't know how to. Their legs were clearly not used to such strenuous activity.

'Hey – you two!' Jamie was yelling from the other end of the corridor. Victoria was with him.

Mr Oak and Mr Quill turned to look, then hurried on. Jamie rushed after them, chasing them into an adjoining corridor. 'You'll not get away from me – you Sassenachs!'

Yelling out his deafening clan war cry, Jamie hurled himself at Mr Quill, dragging him down into a heap on the floor.

Victoria called from a safe distance along the corridor, 'Jamie! Be careful!'

In the pandemonium that followed, Mr Oak stopped momentarily, then hurried off, leaving Mr Quill locked in a wrestling tussle with Jamie on the floor. This continued for several minutes until Jamie finally managed to bend Mr Quill's arm in a vice-like grip behind his back. 'Got you!' Jamie proclaimed triumphantly. But he was horrified to notice that Mr Quill's arm was covered in a hair-like weed formation. In that one moment of distraction, Mr Quill opened his mouth wide, and emitted the loud hissing sound of gas. Jamie took the full force of the fumes, released his grip on Mr Quill's arm, and fell back. Mr Quill seized his opportunity, and tried to make a quick escape. But Jamie grabbed hold of Mr Quill's white jacket, swung him round, and threw a punch at him. All this provoked a piercing scream from Victoria. Mr Quill's entire body seemed to quiver. He clutched his head in agony, and fell to a heap on the floor.

'Jamie!' The Doctor called from the other end of the corridor. Harris was with him.

Jamie recovered himself, wiped his eyes free of the lethal gas fumes, and stood up. 'Well, I took care of him all right,' he said proudly as the Doctor and Harris approached.

The Doctor quickly inspected the slumped and lifeless body of Mr Quill, as Jamie admired his fist which had apparently just numbed Mr Quill. 'There's a wee bit of power in a McCrimmon punch.'

'I'm sorry to disillusion you, Jamie,' said the Doctor, examining Mr Quill's prostrate body, 'but I don't think it was the punch that did it.'

Even as the Doctor was talking, a remarkable physical transformation was taking place in Mr Quill. Jamie and the Doctor watched in amazement as the fern-like fronds on his hands gradually retracted. Whilst this was happening, the

Doctor turned around to give a curious look at Victoria.

'Mr Harris!'

Harris turned with a start to see the Chief Engineer calling from the other end of the corridor.

'You'd better come, sir. The pipeline room!'

The Doctor, Jamie, and Harris reached the pipeline room at exactly the same time as the Chairperson and Perkins. What they found there absolutely shattered them. The transparent section of the pipeline tube was jammed tight with weed clumps and bubbling white foam. And behind it, the thumping, pulsating sound of the alien heartbeat.

'What's happened to it, Doctor?' asked Jamie incredulously.

'It's beginning to expand, the same as it did in the TARDIS.' The Doctor moved a few cautious steps towards the pipeline tube. He was absolutely fascinated with the weed's capacity to reproduce and multiply so much.

Jamie called from a safe distance. 'Is there no way to stop it?'

The Doctor shook his head gravely. 'No. I should have realised this was going to happen.'

Victoria would not enter the room. The squealing mass of weed terrified her, and she was content to watch from the doorway behind the group. What she didn't know was that someone was creeping up behind her in the shadows. Within a few seconds, a weed-covered hand smothered her mouth, and she was dragged out of the room without a sound.

Although the thumping heartbeat sound in the pipeline was muffled, the Chairperson had to raise her voice to be heard. 'Doctor, are you telling us that this horrible stuff – is growing all the time?'

'I'm afraid so,' said the Doctor gloomily. 'In my opinion this is just the start.'

'Mr Harris please! Mr Harris please!' Price's voice was booming out on the tannoy system. 'Chief Robson's broken out of his cabin. He's attacked his Security Guard!'

'What!' Harris yelled back at the tannoy speaker on the wall. 'How the devil did . . . '

'Doctor – look!' Jamie was pointing in horror towards the pipeline tube. The transparent perspex section of the tube had suddenly fractured with a loud crack, right down the centre. This was immediately followed by a surge of white foam, which literally exploded out of the tube onto some of the engineers who were gathered in a group nearby. And behind it, the advance guard of seaweed clumps clearing the way for the quivering tendrils of the giant Weed Creature itself.

'Everybody out! Fast as you can!' The Doctor's shouts now had to compete with the deafening squeals and thumping heartbeat sounds, now released from the confines of the pipeline tube.

The room cleared in double-quick time. But the Chairperson was paralysed with fear, her eyes transfixed on the awesome scene before her, the snake-like tendrils of the Weed Creature stretching out across the room towards her. Everyone was yelling and shouting as they rushed out of the room splattered with foam, and it was left to the Doctor to grab hold of the Chairperson's shoulders and hoist her out of the creature's reach.

Jamie was last to leave. 'Victoria! Where's Victoria?' Jamie's frantic yells seemed to incite the weed and foam into an onslaught of squealing sounds, so he quickly followed the Doctor and Megan Jones out into the Impeller Area, making quite sure the door was firmly closed behind him.

'Where's Victoria?' Jamie asked again anxiously. He and the Doctor looked all around the Area, but Victoria was nowhere to be seen.

'Are you sure she didn't leave with the others?' asked the Doctor.

Jamie had no time to reply. The tannoy speakers were blaring out another emergency message: 'RED ALERT! RED ALERT! DOORS CLOSING!'

The Chairperson made a quick escape back into the

Control Hall, leaving the Doctor and Jamie to continue the search for Victoria in the Impeller Area. 'It's no use,' said the Doctor. 'She's not here!'

The thumping heartbeat sounds were beginning to echo up from the impeller shaft.

'Let's get out of here!' yelled Jamie. He and the Doctor made a dash for the doors of the Control Hall. 'But they were locked.

'Too late!' called the Doctor. He turned, to see a red light flashing above the doors leading to the Compound corridor. 'They're closing too! This way! Hurry!'

They retreated from the Impeller Area just in time. The whole place was filling up with lethal gas fumes.

Not so far away, another red alarm light was flashing. This time it was above a door leading to the sea front. Robson appeared in the corridor leading to the exit. He was carrying the unconscious Victoria across his shoulder. As he reached the exit, a klaxon horn suddenly screeched out on the wall above him. Robson wasted no time. Within a few seconds he was gone, taking his hostage with him.

The sound of klaxon horns was now echoing throughout the Refinery. Emergency procedures were in operation as crewmen rushed in and out of the Control Hall on full alert. The whole place was buzzing with frenzied activity.

'Pipeline Room!' Harris was yelling to two engineers from the steps leading up to the inspection area. 'Seal it off! Quick as you can!' The two men raced out of the Hall, leaving Harris to yell at another engineer, this time at one of the control gauges. 'Close all pipelines – in and out!' The engineer looked at him in utter bewilderment. 'Come on, man!' Harris had never spoken so aggressively to anyone in his whole life. 'What the hell are you waiting for?' The engineer immediately obeyed, quickly turning pressure wheels, levers, and other instruments on the control panel.

Meanwhile, the Chairperson went to Price at the Control Cone. 'Any news of Robson?' she asked.

'Not yet, madam. We've got a full alert out on him.'

The Chairperson was not satisfied. 'Get on to Security!' she demanded. 'Tell them to search everywhere. Whatever happens – they *must* find Chief Robson!'

Somewhere along a snow-covered cliff top near the Refinery, a Minimoke bicycle car was racing much too fast on the icy road. At the wheel was the deranged figure of Robson, with Victoria slumped unconscious on the seat behind him.

The Minimoke came to a halt in a clearing at the top of the cliff. Robson got out, dragged Victoria from the back seat, and threw her across his shoulder. He turned, and quickly made his way to another vehicle that was waiting for him.

It was a helicopter.

11

The Nerve Centre

The central video monitor at the Control Cone suddenly buzzed with activity. Price swung round on his seat and called out across the Hall excitedly, 'Mr Harris!'

Harris rushed across from the office area immediately, 'What have you got?'

'It's Chief Robson, sir! He's just taking off.'

'Taking off?' Harris looked at the video monitor. One of the Company's two-seater British Aerospace helicopters was just rising up from the chopper pad at the top of the cliffs. As it quickly gained height, a great white spray of snow rose with it from the down draught.

Harris watched the screen in despair for a moment or so, then growled, 'Keep a close track on that chopper. Don't let it out of your sight!'

In the Compound corridor just outside the Control Hall, Jamie found himself caught up in the chaos as engineers rushed up and down in general emergency. The weed enemy had penetraded the very heart of the Euro-Gas network, and from now on it was every man for himself.

151

'Victoria?' Jamie was desperately stopping every engineer who bumped into him. 'Have you seen Victoria!' Each time the answer was the same, an impatient shaking of the head followed by a mad dash to get out of the place. Jamie was practically beside himself, when the Doctor suddenly appeared at the end of the corridor. 'Doctor! Have you found her?'

'She's gone!' said the Doctor breathlessly, as he rushed forward to meet Jamie. 'I've been right the way round.'

'But she was standing right beside us.'

'Doctor!' Harris was calling from the door of the Control Hall. 'Robson's trying to get away in one of the Company helicopters.'

'Blast!' The Doctor moved briskly towards the Control Hall. 'I should have known!'

Harris stopped him briefly at the door. 'I'm afraid he's got your young girl with him.'

The Doctor looked up sharply in horror. Then he turned to Jamie.

'Oh no!' The young Highland warrior looked utterly crushed.

By the time the Doctor, Jamie, and Harris reached the video monitor at the Control Cone, Robson's blue and white helicopter showing the legend *EURO-GAS* in huge black letters, was soaring off into the distance out to sea.

A small group, including the Chairperson and Perkins, gathered around the Cone. 'Is there any way of speaking to Robson from here?' the Doctor asked Harris.

Harris turned to Price at the Control panel. 'Switch to RT.' Price flicked a switch and a green transmitting light appeared above the video monitor. Harris turned back to the Doctor, and said, 'Go ahead.'

The Doctor spoke directly to the video monitor. 'Robson, are you there? Robson, can you hear me?'

At the helicopter controls, Robson jumped with a start as he suddenly heard the Doctor's voice booming out through the RT unit.

'Robson! This is the Doctor. Listen to me. *Please* listen! Come back to the Refinery, Robson. Do you hear me? Come back!'

The Doctor's distorted voice was clearly causing Robson a great deal of pain. His face crumpled up, and he clutched one of his ears in agony.

The Doctor tried again. 'Robson! Don't you understand? They're trying to control you. They want to use you as a weapon against us. Resist them, Robson! You are part of the human race. You *are* one of us. Do you hear me, Robson. *You are one of us . . .* '

Robson grabbed the RT microphone and flicked a switch. But when he tried to speak, the words would just not form in his mouth. 'L-l-l-listen . . . ' he sluttered. 'L-l-l-listen – to – me . . . '

There was a deadly silence throughout the Control Hall as everyone listened to the faint, barely audible, amost robotic voice of Robson, filtering through static from the central video monitor.

'The girl . . . I have the girl . . . my prisoner . . . my hostage . . . '

The Chairperson suddenly bellowed at the monitor. 'Robson! This is Megan! Don't be a fool, man . . . !'

'Quite please!' the Doctor demanded angrily. 'Let him finish!'

Robson continued. 'The girl . . . if you want her to live . . . you must come . . . you must come over – to us . . . ' His voice gradually trailed away, and finally disappeared.

'Robson!' called the Doctor. 'Robson, can you hear me?'

Price turned from the Control panel. 'We've lost him, sir. He must have switched off.'

'What did he mean?' asked the Chairperson. 'Come over to us?'

'Exactly what he said,' replied the Doctor tersely.

Harris looked anxiously at the Doctor. 'You mean – they want *you*?'

The Doctor smiled knowingly. 'Oh yes. They obviously realise I am a threat to them.'

'But you won't go – surely?'

Everyone was watching the Doctor tensely, waiting for his reply.

'Of course I shall go!'

There were shocked murmurs all around the Hall. Some of them were of consternation, others were of admiration.

The Chairperson had to raise her voice to be heard above the din. 'But we need you here. You're our only hope!'

'If I stay here,' the Doctor assured her, 'that hope will be very slim indeed.'

Now Jamie stepped forward. 'Doctor, don't let that madman take Victoria. We've got to stop him!'

'You two are the mad ones if you go chasing after Robson,' insisted the Chairperson. 'You can see for your-self, he's a danger to everyone.'

The Doctor appreciated the Chairperson's sudden concern, but his mind was made up. 'No, Jamie's right,' he said. 'We've got to go after him.'

'There's a Company helicopter,' said Harris. 'We'll have a pilot waiting for you.'

'Thank you,' smiled the Doctor, as he and Jamie made their way to the Compound exit door. But they stopped abruptly as they heard the Chairperson shouting at Harris across the Hall.

'Harris! If we let this man go now, what hope have we?'

The Doctor answered her. 'The only hope you have, madam, is that my hunch is proved correct.'

'Hunch?'

'That Mr Robson will lead us straight to the nerve centre of the weed colony.'

Robson's blue and white-coloured helicopter was almost invisible against the grim, grey winter sky. But the cracking sound of the chopper's blades were sharp enough to disperse any stray seagull that had been left behind by the mass migration of seabirds from the eastern seaboard of the English coast.

At the controls of the helicopter, Robson was quite oblivious to what was happening to him. He had become a mere instrument of the weed's mental control over him. He was no longer capable, or indeed permitted, to think for himself.

Down below, the mud-coloured sea was pitted with undulating swells of white spray and bubbling blobs of foam, soon to become a slave of the fury from the deep . . .

Back on the mainland, another, somewhat larger Company helicopter was taking off from the chopper pad at the top of the cliffs. This time the passengers were the Doctor and Jamie, who were well wrapped up against the cold in Company regulation anoraks. Flying in a helicopter was a whole new experience for Jamie. Although in some ways it resembled travel in the TARDIS, he was particularly fascinated by the manoeuverability of the machine, especially when it skimmed just above the waves.

Because of the piercing noise created by the helicopter's huge rotating blades, the Doctor and the pilot had agreed to communicate with each other by means of sign language – pointing up, pointing down, and this way, that way, and so on.

After consulting the map, the Doctor still had no idea which direction they should be making for. In his estimation, the nerve centre of the weed colony could be just about anywhere, and it was going to be like searching for a needle in a haystack. At this stage also, he had no idea that Robson was heading out to sea. So, tapping the pilot at his side on the arm, the Doctor pointed to a direction which he chose as the result of a hunch.

The pilot took the helicopter up to an operational height, then headed off into a north-easterly direction, straight along the coastline.

* * *

The central video monitor at the Control Cone was relaying pictures from the Refinery's radar system. Harris, the Chairperson, and Perkins were absorbed with a small yellow dot on the screen's tracking diagram, which represented the position of Robson's helicopter out at sea.

Price suddenly interrupted them. He had picked up a message through his earphones. 'Mr Harris, sir! The Doctor is airborne.'

'Right! Put him through on RT.' Harris waited for Price to flick a switch, then talked directly to the video monitor. 'Doctor, this is Harris. Can you hear me? Over!'

The Doctor's voice came booming through the tannoy speakers loud and clear. 'I hear you, Mr Harris. Go ahead please. Over!'

'Listen to me, Doctor. Can you see Robson yet?'

'No – not a sign.'

'Right, now listen carefully.' Harris brushed the lock of hair from his eye and spoke urgently. 'We've managed to track Robson on the Radarscope. He's landed on the Control Rig Complex. Can you hear me? The Control Rig Complex. Over!'

There was a moment's hesitation, then the Doctor answered in a very excited voice. 'The Control Rig! Well, well, well. So that's the nerve centre.'

The Chairperson was straining to hear the Doctor's reply. 'What did he say? Ask him to repeat.'

Harris called back to the monitor. 'Say again please, Doctor! Say again! Over!'

The Doctor's voice boomed back through the tannoy speakers immediately. 'I said, we're on our way to the Control Rig. Over and out!'

The RT link-up came to an end, and Harris turned from the monitor with a grave expression.

The Chairperson said, 'What chance have they got?'

'Your guess is as good as mine,' sighed Harris.

'So what do we do now?'

'We sit and wait.' Harris flopped down into the nearest

chair, and covered his face with his hands. He was exhausted – and pessimistic. 'If the Doctor hasn't done something within an hour, I'm evacuating the Compound.'

The Chairperson thumped her fist angrily into the palm of her other hand. 'No!' she growled. 'I forbid it!'

Harris looked up and glared straight at her defiantly. 'And that's final – Miss Jones!'

The Chairperson was outraged. But she didn't say another word.

The North Sea had never looked more menacing. A few miles from the mainland great tufts of thick grey cloud hung over the surface of the water, each of them looking like the distorted faces of goblins, relishing the thought of what was to come.

The blue and white Euro-Gas helicopter carrying the Doctor and Jamie darted in and out of the clouds, dispersing them into even more grotesque shapes. The search for Robson and Victoria was intensifying, and their destination, the Control Rig Complex, was positioned in the middle of the network of gas rigs some twenty miles out from the coastline.

Their first sign that they were approaching the rigs was when Jamie caught sight of a yellow rubber dingy bobbing up and down on the rolling waves. Then the Doctor picked out another one, and then another. Soon, the entire area was littered with identical survival craft, all bearing the Euro-Gas legend. Each one of them was empty. The Doctor's worst fears were confirmed. The weed was permitting no-one to escape from its massive onslaught.

Soon after they passed over the dinghies, the pilot suddenly drew the Doctor's attention to something down below and dead ahead. It was their first view of the vast complex of rigs, jutting out of the sea and mist like huge ghostly galleons. The largest construction was the Control Rig complex itself. This was surrounded at a distance by a rectangle of smaller rigs, all of them containing chopper pads with EG printed in bold black letters. The Doctor pointed downwards, and the pilot began descending the helicopter.

The helicopter approached the rigs at low level, skimming just above the surface of the waves. Jamie felt a mixture of exhilaration and anxiety as they weaved in and out of the rigs. They were barren, unwelcoming places for human beings to spend so much time on, boasting nothing more than cranes, hoists, and a massive web of drilling machinery. And as they drew closer, the full impact of what had happened to the rigs and its crew, became a frightening reality. Every one of the rigs and the sea around was covered with a layer of bubbling white foam. The effect was dazzling. In the Doctor's mind, he and Jamie were two flies being enticed into a giant spider's web.

Within a few moments, the helicopter was hovering over the Control Rig, and the huge rotating blades soon dispersed the foam below, propelling huge blobs of it into the air. The helicopter door opened, and Jamie threw out a rope ladder which reached down to the chopper pad.

The Doctor was first to climb down the ladder, then Jamie. It was a perilous descent, for the pad had been left slippery by the alien foam. Once they were safely down, the Doctor turned to look up and give the pilot the thumbs-up sign. The pilot did likewise, withdrew the ladder, and took the helicopter up to a higher altitude.

'Over her, Jamie!' called the Doctor, as he found his way to a steel door marked *LOG ROOM. AUTHORISED PERSONNEL ONLY*.

Jamie followed quickly, but stopped briefly to take a suspicious look around the ghost-like rig. 'Where *is* everyone?' he said. 'The place is deserted.'

The Doctor used both hands to open the heavy steel door. 'Careful now, Jamie. We're being watched.' Without another word, he disappeared through the door. Jamie lingered just long enough to notice the lack of seabirds everywhere. His eyes were very firmly directed towards the helicopter, hovering above the rig.

Then he too quickly disappeared through the door. After he was gone, the white blobs of foam began to reform.

The Doctor and Jamie found themselves at the top of a flight of metal steps which led down to a poorly lit corridor, containing not one door, but three.

'So far, so good,' said the Doctor quietly.

'Will the driver wait for us?' asked Jamie hopefully.

The Doctor smiled. 'The driver is not a driver, Jamie. He's a pilot. Don't worry, he'll wait.'

Jamie swallowed hard and looked at the corridor below. 'Do we go down there?'

'I'm afraid so. Follow me.'

Jamie kept as close behind the Doctor as he possibly could. 'It's like walking into the lion's den.'

'I feel we're already in his den, Jamie. We must just try to avoid putting our heads into his mouth!'

Their slow, cautious footsteps echoed on the metal steps, until finally they were in the corridor below, which was just above sea-level.

'It's awful quiet,' whispered Jamie. 'You think Victoria's down here?'

'I don't know. It's possible.'

Without stopping to think, Jamie suddenly called out to Victoria in exactly the same way he had done so many times before during their adventures together. 'Victoria! Where are you?'

The Doctor immediately clapped his hand over Jamie's mouth. 'Ssh, Jamie! There'll be no element of surprise . . . '

No sooner had he spoken than Victoria's stifled voice came echoing from somewhere along the corridor. 'Jamie! Doctor!'

Jamie pulled the Doctor's hand away from his mouth. 'It's her! It's Victoria!' He was about to move off in the direction of Victoria's call, when the Doctor quickly stopped him.

'Wait Jamie!'

'What's the matter?'

'If you were hunting, what would you do?'

Jamie thought for a moment. 'Oh Aye. It could be a trap?'

The Doctor nodded. 'Let's be cautious, just in case.' He and Jamie moved slowly along the corridor.

They paused briefly outside the first door, then after a moment's hesitation, they barged straight in. The Doctor turned on the light. It was a small video and computer tape store cupboard. But no Victoria. They repeated the process at the next door. This time it was the Log Room itself. But once again, although deserted in a hurry, everything was in order. And still no sign of Victoria.

As they approached the third door, they stopped dead. They could hear the slow, pulsating sound of the alien heartbeat coming from inside the room.

The Doctor looked at Jamie. 'This must be it. Ready?'

Jamie gulped hard, then nodded. The Doctor carefully opened the door. The heartbeat sound stopped immediately. The room was in darkness. Jamie felt for the light switch, and flicked it on.

The room exploded into a cacophony of squeals and deafening, pulsating heartbeat sounds.

The Doctor and Jamie stared in horror as the room was flooded with light. They were in a large crew cabin, at the far end of which was a seething mass of bubbling white foam. And in the midst of that foam was a sight that would chill the blood of even the strongest of mortals. The figure of a man was standing there, half-demented, his neck and hands sprouting frond-like weed formations. And out of the foam that had almost completely engulfed him, the curling tentacles of the giant Weed Creature were snaking around his lifeless body.

The deafening heartbeat sound stopped abruptly. There was a deathly silence, then the man who had become a creature himself, began to emerge from the foam, arms outstretched, walking slowly, jerkily, straight towards the Doctor and Jamie.

'Come in, Doctor,' whispered the human creature. 'We've been waiting for you . . .'

It was Robson.

12

'Scream, Victoria! Scream!'

The pilot of the Euro-Gas Company helicopter peered down at the incredible phenomenon in the sea beneath him. The platform and chopper pad of the Control Rig were almost totally engulfed in bubbling white foam, presenting a dazzling spectacle from the air.

It had all happened so quickly. Within moments of the Doctor and Jamie disappearing from view below the platform, the alien foam had quickly regathered and asserted its superiority. Hovering in the sky high above the North Sea, the pilot was convinced that he would never see any sign of human life on that rig again. All he could do now was to watch, wait, and speculate on what grim horrors were being played out within the bowels of that doom-laden mausoleum in the middle of the sea . . .

'What do you want of me?' The Doctor was backing away from the deformed human creature that was Robson, who was advancing on him and Jamie from a mass of bubbling white foam.

Robson, arms outstretched as though reaching out to touch the Doctor, came to a halt. His eyes were glazed over with a thin white film, and he was breathless, barely audible. 'You – are going to help – our new masters.' His voice was slow, disjointed. 'They need you.'

'Need me?' The Doctor was suspicious, but fascinated by Robson's reply.

Suddenly they were interrupted by the sound of someone banging at a door along the corridor outside.

'Jamie! Doctor! Down here!' It was Victoria, her voice muffled, but yelling her head off. 'Get me out of here!'

'Victoria!' Jamie immediately dashed out of the room to look for her, leaving the Doctor to face the zombie-like creature alone.

'You . . . are going to help . . . with the conquest . . . of the human planet.' Robson's mouth seemed to move almost mechanically.

'Robson, listen to me!' The Doctor began to play for time. 'Can't you see what they've done to you? The weed is evil, Robson. It is dominating your mind . . . '

'The human mind . . . is now obsolete. It is . . . tired. It is . . . dead.' Robson started to move again. 'Only our new masters . . . can offer us . . . life!'

'Matter will never conquer mind, Robson. It's against the law of nature.' The Doctor had now backed into the open doorway. As he did so, he just caught a glimpse of Jamie throwing himself against the door of another room in the corridor outside. But he quickly turned back to Robson, who was now only a few metres away from him. 'Don't you care what they've done to you, Robson? Don't you care what they've done to your body?'

'The body . . . does not exist. Soon . . . ' – Robson opened his arms wide as though intending to embrace the Doctor – ' . . . we shall all . . . be one!' As soon as he had finished speaking, he opened his mouth wide and leaned directly towards the Doctor. The sound of hissing toxic gas came from the back of his throat.

The Doctor quickly shielded his face with his hands, then yelled out into the corridor. 'Victoria! Jamie! Hurry!'

With one last supreme effort, Jamie threw himself against the door of the room where Victoria was being held hostage, and burst it open.

'No escape . . . ' continued Robson breathlessly. 'We are . . . the new masters . . . join us . . . join us . . . you will . . . join us . . . '

Robson, arms outstretched again, started to advance on the Doctor. The Doctor made a quick dash for the corridor, where Jamie and Victoria were just coming out of the room where the girl had been held hostage.

'Out!' yelled the Doctor. 'Both of you. Fast as you can!'

Jamie shouted back, and pointed frantically. 'Doctor! Behind you!' The Doctor turned. Robson was in the corridor, and closing in on him.

As soon as she saw the horrible deformed sight that was Robson, Victoria screamed.

Robson stopped dead, as though he had suddenly been shot. He clutched his ears in agony, and whilst the Doctor, Jamie, and Victoria looked on in absolute amazement, he began to writhe and squirm with pain, groaning, 'No . . . no . . . no . . . no . . . '

It was at that crucial moment that, for the first time, the Doctor discovered the secret of the alien weed's vulnerability. Turning quickly to Victoria, his face beaming with excitement, he yelled, 'Scream, Victoria! *Scream*!'

Victoria, trembling with fear behind Jamie, was bewildered. 'What?' she asked. 'What do you mean?'

'Do as I say, Victoria!' demanded the Doctor, jumping up and down impatiently. 'Scream again!'

Victoria duly obliged. Nobody could scream with such intensity as she, and the noise she made practically rocked the very foundation of the rig.

'No!' Robson couldn't bear the sound piercing through his head, and started to retreat backwards into the Log Room. As he did so, the small blobs of foam that had been clinging to him, disintegrated. 'Stop! Stop!' he called, but his pleas were barely audible.

'Come on, Victoria!' The Doctor grabbed hold of Victoria's hand and led her to the Log Room. Jamie followed them. All three stood in the open doorway, watching Robson retreat back into the seething mass of bubbling white foam at the other end of the cabin. 'Keep screaming, Victoria!' cried the Doctor. And once again, Victoria obliged.

Robson was now demented by the noise. Clutching his ears in agony, struggling to breathe, he sunk lower and lower into the foam, groaning inaudibly, 'No . . . No . . . ' And just near him, the curling tentacles of the giant Weed Creature quivered frantically, desperately trying to hold on to the power that was gradually ebbing away from it. Within a matter of moments, Robson had been completely engulfed by the foam.

'Now's our chance!' said the Doctor urgently. 'Let's get out of here!'

All three hurried along the corridor and began climbing the steps leading up to the rig platform. Victoria turned briefly. 'Jamie! We didn't lock the room!'

Jamie started to turn back, but the Doctor stopped him. 'Leave it, Jamie! Leave it! There's no time!'

The Doctor pushed Jamie up the steps, then quickly followed him. Once he had reached the platform door, he turned briefly to look back down at the corridor below. The bubbling white foam was beginning to seep out from the Log Room.

The air above the surface of the Control Rig was crisp and clear after the choking, gas-filled atmosphere of the corridors below. A calm breeze was rapidly building up into a full-blown gale, whipping the sea into a frenzy of activity.

Victoria hesitated at the steel surface door, too terrified to move. All around her, the platform area was almost completely covered in bubbling white foam.

'It's all right, Victoria,' said Jamie, putting a reassuring arm around her shoulders. 'It doesna' harm you.'

As soon as the Doctor appeared at the door, the deafening

165

sound of the thumping, alien heartbeat echoed up from the corridor below. 'Quick, Jamie! Help me bolt the door!' Using all the strength in their shoulders, they managed to close the heavy steel door, immediately cutting off the sound of the heartbeat. After they had pushed the huge bolt back into position, the Doctor breathed a sigh of relief. 'That should hold them for a bit!'

Jamie looked at him with a puzzled start. 'Them?' he asked.

The Doctor waded off a little into the foam, which was now up to his waist. 'Where the devil's that helicopter?' he called, looking all around the sky above the rig. He suddenly spotted it, 'Ah – there!' He was pointing to something which appeared as no more than a small speck, hovering just below the clouds some distance away.

'Hey! Down here!' Jamie, Victoria, and the Doctor started waving madly at the helicopter.

'What's the matter with him?' yelled Jamie.

'Can't he see us?' yelled Victoria.

The Doctor stopped waving. 'Probably not. There's too much foam.'

'More likely he's just scared!' Jamie was now waving both his hands.

All three suddenly turned with a start. There was a loud thumping, banging sound on the heavy steel door they had just bolted.

'Let's get out of here!' called the Doctor urgently. 'We can't wait for the helicopter.'

Jamie thought the Doctor had gone stark raving mad. 'But we can't get off this rig without it.'

'Oh yes we can!' The Doctor pointed to something that was protruding out of the foam on the chopper pad. It was the small helicopter Robson had used for kidnapping Victoria.

Jamie stared in horror at the tiny machine. 'But there's no pilot!'

'And it's only got two seats!' added Victoria.

166

'Two seats are better than none, my dear,' replied the Doctor with a grin. 'And anyway, I've been dying to get my hands on one of those things . . .' The banging on the heavy steel door became more intense, more forceful. Someone was determined to break it down. 'No time to lose!' yelled the Doctor. 'Come on!'

The Doctor rushed off into the foam, leaving Jamie and Victoria to exchange a look of total horror at what they were letting themselves into. But as the steel door began to show signs of giving way, Jamie grabbed hold of Victoria's hand, and dragged her through the foam towards the chopper pad.

Within a few minutes, the Doctor, Jamie, and Victoria were crammed inside the cockpit of the tiny helicopter. The foam was expanding rapidly, and creeping up the sides of the windows. If the three companions were to make their escape, this was their last chance to do so.

'Doctor, are you sure you know how to fly one of these things?' asked Jamie, nervously.

'Nothing to it, my boy,' replied the Doctor, wildly flicking every switch he could lay his hands on. 'I watched the pilot on the way over.'

Victoria's eyes widened in horror. 'You mean, this is the first time you've been in one of these machines?'

'Don't worry,' said the Doctor confidently, 'this is a very primitive machine. It's quite simple to control – once you know how to . . .'

By sheer luck rather than skill, the Doctor pressed one particular computer button which suddenly sent the helicopter's blades whirring into action above their heads. 'Ah!' he exclaimed, rubbing his hands triumphantly, 'now for lift-off!'

'Doctor, look!'

Through the window, Jamie could see someone, arms outstretched, struggling towards the helicopter through the whirling clouds of foam. It was Robson. Behind him were a group of other zombie-like human figures, all sprouting weed formations from their necks and arms. One of them was a woman.

Jamie could hardly believe his eyes. 'It's Robson . . . and Mrs Harris . . . and there's van Lutyens . . . there's a whole lot of them!'

Victoria became almost hysterical. 'Hurry, Doctor! Hurry!'

The Doctor was still negotiating the computer controls, undecided which button or switch would activate the helicopter into a lift-off. 'Now, let me see,' he mumbled, 'is it this one . . . or maybe it's . . . '

'*Doctor*!' Jamie was yelling at the top of his voice, for Robson and the other zombies were gradually closing in on them.

The Doctor was still fumbling with the controls. 'Nearly there, Jamie! Nearly there . . . '

Victoria shrieked. The faces of Robson, Maggie Harris, and the other human Weed Creatures were pressed up against the windows of the helicopter, clawing with their hands to get in.

'Do something, Doctor! Hurry!'

Almost as Jamie was yelling, the Doctor found the computer button he was looking for, and the helicopter rose up from the chopper pad, scattering white foam into the air. The take-off was not exactly a perfect one, for the machine seemed briefly to veer sideways rather than upwards, narrowly missing the rig's main observation tower.

Jamie and Victoria, squeezed onto the front seat of the helicopter at the side of the Doctor, clung desperately to each other for protection. Eventually however, the machine did begin to rise, and the last view they had of the control rig below was of Robson and the other human Weed Creatures, all grouped together on the chopper pad, arms outstretched, as though reaching out in desolation towards the sky.

'Right!' said the Doctor, impressed with his own mastery of the helicopter's controls. 'Let's get back to the Refinery . . . ' But as he pressed the steering stick he was clutching, the machine veered off at an acute angle, and started to plunge towards the sea.

Jamie and Victoria were scared stiff and yelling their heads off. 'Doctor! What are you doing? Up, Doctor! *Up*!'

The Doctor was in a complete flap at the controls. 'Oh dear, I seem to have . . . '

He was suddenly interrupted by a voice coming through the helicopter's RT system. It was the pilot of the other Euro-Gas helicopter who was tailing them nearby. 'Euro-Gas One to Euro-Gas Three. Having trouble? Heave back on your stick and increase your throttle!'

The Doctor called back: 'Are you sure that's right?'

Jamie and Victoria shouted at him in unison. 'Doctor! Do as he says!'

The Euro-Gas pilot watched with relief as the Doctor's helicopter pulled out of its dive just as it was about to hit the water. Then it started to climb and level out.

The Doctor turned to his two terrified companions and smiled confidently at them. Then he talked to the other pilot through the RT unit. 'Thank you so much for your help. I've got the machine off the ground and it should be comparatively simple to propel it forward. However, there is just one thing . . . ' He paused, glanced guiltily at Jamie and Victoria, then continued: 'How do I land it?'

Jamie and Victoria exchanged a look of agony.

Back at the Refinery, the Control Hall was like a tomb. At the Cone, Harris, Megan Jones, Perkins and Price were watching the video monitor screens for news of the Doctor. But all the equipment remained ominously silent. Everyone had the same feeling of impending doom.

'It's no good!' growled Harris, suddenly thumping the desk in front of him, 'it's quite obvious we're not going to hear from the Doctor or any of them again. We *must* evacuate the Compound!'

'No, Harris!' insisted the Chairperson, straightening up in her chair. 'We said an hour. He has ten more minutes.'

'But even if he does come back, what can he do? The only possible weapon we might have used against the weed has been destroyed.'

'You're quite sure we've lost the entire stock of oxygen?'

'Every cylinder.'

'Right!' The Chairperson rose quickly from her seat, and turned to her secretary. 'Perkins, get on to London. Inform the Defence Minister I want a full red alert on this now. Tell him what's happened, and ask him to arrange for as many tankers of oxygen as he can muster to be sent here immediately.'

'Yes, madam!' The bewildered Perkins swung back to Price to put the call through the London. You could tell he was disorientated by all that had happened: his tie was crooked.

'They won't be in time,' warned Harris. He and the Chairperson were strolling back towards the Office Area together. 'Our only hope now is to evacuate the Compound. The Pipeline Room is a mass of weed and foam. You've seen how rapidly it reproduces. It could swamp us all at any time.'

'It could, but it hasn't yet.' The Chairperson was becoming irritated with Harris again. 'Until it does,' she said firmly, 'we stay here!'

Harris responded icily. 'And when it does attack, how do you expect to fight it? With what weapons?'

'Perhaps *I* can answer that question.'

Everyone turned to find out who was speaking. It was the Doctor, who was just entering the hall. With him were Jamie and Victoria, looking decidedly fragile after their hair-raising ordeal in the helicopter.

'Doctor! You're alive!' The Chairperson immediately went to meet him. 'What about Robson? Did you find him?'

'My wife!' Harris asked eagerly. 'What about my wife?'

'We found your wife, Mr Harris,' replied the Doctor solemnly. 'And Mr Robson.'

'Aye. And a lot of other people too,' added Jamie.

'Are they – alive?' asled the Chairperson timorously.

The Doctor nodded. 'Yes, they're alive. But only just. They're being held hostage out at the Control Rig, under the mental and physical control of the Weed?'

Harris was shattered. 'Then I was right. There's no hope. No hope at all.'

'You're wrong, Mr Harris,' said the Doctor objectively. 'I believe there *is* hope.'

'But even if we succeed in fighting off the Weed, what about . . . my wife, Maggie . . . all those people affected by it?'

The Doctor suddenly became very positive. 'On our way back here, we stopped at the Medicare Unit. The man Jamie fought with in the corridor has almost completely recovered.'

'What!'

'The weed growth on him has disappeared, shrivelled up and died. The man is still confused and dazed – but he's alive!'

'But . . . how? Why? What killed the Weed?'

The Doctor smiled, and wagged his finger. 'A very good question, Mr Harris. But I think I know the answer.' He hesitated. 'It was noise!'

Everyone in the hall turned to look at him in absolute astonishment.

'Noise?' asked Harris incredulously.

The Chairperson was puzzled. 'You mean, *noise* can actually kill the Weed?'

'Not any type of noise, Miss Jones,' explained the Doctor, 'a particular pattern of sound vibrations.' Then he turned to Victoria who was standing just behind him. 'Actually, it was my young friend here who discovered it.'

'Me!' spluttered Victoria, astonished.

The Doctor smiled gratefully. 'You screamed, my dear.'

'I screamed?' For a moment, Victoria was puzzled. But gradually, a smile of comprehension showed on her face. 'Oh, yes – I screamed.'

The Doctor turned back to Harris and the Chairperson.

'You see, it is Victoria's own particular pattern of sound that seems to do the trick. The Weed's nerve system is clearly hyper-sensitive to it.'

'I'm not surprised,' muttered Jamie under his breath to Victoria. 'So am I!' Victoria retaliated by stamping on his toe.

'So that's why the crews on the rigs spoke softly,' suggested Harris. 'Certain types of noise affected them.'

'Very possibly, Mr Harris,' replied the Doctor. 'And in my opinion, that is the most important clue we've had so far.'

The Chairperson's spirits were beginning to revive. 'So where do we go from here, Doctor?'

'Before you evacuate this area, will you give me half-an-hour?' he asked.

Harris shook his head anxiously. 'The risk is too great. The whole refinery is crawling with seaweed.'

'Half-an-hour won't make that much difference,' insisted the Chairperson. 'Doctor, what d'you think we can do?'

'We make a noise, Miss Jones – an awful lot of noise.'

Again Harris shook his head. 'We're too late. We'll never stop the Weed now.'

'We've got to!' said the Doctor forcefully. 'There may not be another chance.'

'It's impossible, I tell you. The foam is seeping in from every corner of the Compound.'

'What we need to do is to attack its nerve centre.'

Now the Chairperson was doubtful. 'But you said yourself, we don't know where the nerve centre is.'

The Doctor's eyes lit up. 'Ah – but we do!' He turned to look up at the illuminated rig guide at the top of the Cone, and pointed to the Control Rig light. 'There!'

'That's the Control Rig,' said Harris.

'Precisely! We must generate enough sound to penetrate through to the Control Rig.'

'Easier said than done,' said the Chairperson. 'How do we get it there?'

172

They were suddenly interrupted by a sound coming from the pipeline tube above their heads. Everyone in the hall stopped what they were doing and turned to stare at the giant tube. The sound was unmistakeable. Squeals, scratching, bubbling, and the thumping, pulsating heartbeat of the Weed itself.

'That's how!' yelled the Doctor above the sound, pointing to, and carrying his glance along the pipeline tube around the hall. 'We'll transmit all the noise we can to the Control Rig – through the pipeline.' He turned back to Harris, who was again shaking his head warily. 'Mr Harris, this is the only way of saving your wife – and everyone else!'

Harris still resisted. 'Yes, I realise that, but – '

'Half-an-hour, Mr Harris, that's all.'

Harris, torn by indecision, stared hard at the Doctor for a moment. Then he moved quickly to the Control Cone. 'Price! Let me see what's happening in the pipeline room.'

Price flicked a switch and the huge central video monitor screen sprang into life. There was an immediate gasp from everyone in the hall. The screen showed the pipeline room, now completely engulfed in a seething mass of bubbling white foam and squealing, wriggling weed tentacles.

Harris, although shaken, spoke quickly, urgently. 'Half-an-hour? Yes, that's about all the time we've got.' Then he swung back to the Doctor. 'But you're right – we *must* try!'

'Right! Let's get started!' The Doctor immediately became very busy, inspecting the electrical circuits at the Cone. 'Where are all these wires connected to?'

Price answered. 'Transmitter and loudspeaker system underneath.' He watched in bewilderment as the Doctor followed the path of the wiring to the back of the Cone equipment. 'Doctor, what's this all about?'

The Doctor was thinking rather than answering Price's question. 'If we can boost this equipment to transmit enough sound through the pipeline, we can destroy the weed's nerve centre.'

The Chairperson was watching the Doctor's bustling activity as though he were quite mad. 'Do you really think this idea will work?'

The Doctor, who had briefly disappeared behind the control panel, suddenly popped his head up again to ask: 'Mr Price, have you a tape-recording machine or some such instrument? It needs to be quite a powerful one.'

'Yes, sir!' Price flicked more switches, then swung round in his seat to pull down an overhead snake microphone. 'Ready when you are, Doctor!'

The Doctor called, 'Over here, Victoria – hurry now!'

Victoria rushed across to the Cone, looking very worried about the whole thing. The Doctor took her hand, patted it reassuringly and said, 'I want you to scream as loud as you can for Mr Price. He's going to record it. All right?'

Victoria bit her lower lip nervously and replied, 'If you say so, Doctor.'

The Doctor smiled, then quickly turned to Price. 'Make a loop of the recording so that we can repeat it continuously,' he said.

Price nodded, then adjusted the microphone to suit Victoria's height. The Doctor rubbed his hands together excitedly, then bustled off towards the engineers over on the control platforms.

'I hope he knows what he's doing,' sighed the Chairperson.

Jamie answered her indignantly. 'Of course the Doctor knows what he's doing!' But he had second thoughts, and added, 'At least, I think he does . . . '

'Mr Harris!' The Chief Engineer was calling from the door of the impeller area. 'The shaft!'

Harris exchanged a quick look of alarm with the Chairperson, then hurried across to the impeller area.

The Chairperson went straight to the Doctor, who was concealed on the floor behind the Cone, sorting out a vast complex of cables and electronic equipment. 'Doctor,' she said urgently, 'we must hurry!'

In the impeller area the thumping, pulsating heartbeat sound was deafening. By the time Harris and the Chief Engineer rushed in, a flood of foam and weed had seeped up from the lift shaft, and was swirling around inside the airlock.

Back in the Control Hall, the Doctor was feverishly dismantling four magnetised loudspeakers from the back of the Cone. Then he turned to a group of engineers watching him tensely nearby: 'Somebody take these speakers and attach them at intervals along the pipeline!'

There was a rush of volunteers, who took off with the speakers, each one trailing its own cable behind it.

Meanwhile, Price finished preparing the tape recording equipment for Victoria, who was very unnerved by the thought that the survival of the human race might depend on her scream.

'Right, Miss,' said Price, adjusting the microphone one last time, 'the moment I give the signal, scream your head off.' Victoria nodded, and waited for the signal. When it came, she opened her mouth, then hesitated. Price signalled again. Victoria shook her head. She seemed mesmerised by the microphone dangling in front of her. Price was getting frantic. 'Go ahead, Miss,' he urged, 'the tape's running!' Victoria again shook her head. She was in a panic. 'I can't! I don't know why – but I just can't!'

'What's the matter?' asked the Doctor impatiently as he joined them.

Price swivelled around on his chair. 'The young lady, sir. She can't scream.'

'*Can't scream*!' spluttered the Doctor. He knew many things about Victoria, one of which was that she had the loudest, most terrifying scream he had ever heard. 'Victoria,' he said scoldingly, 'this is ridiculous!'

Victoria was nearly in tears. 'I'm sorry, Doctor – I just don't know why I can't do it. I think . . . I think I'm too . . .' Her eyes widened as she suddenly caught sight of something over the Doctor's shoulders. On the other side of the Hall,

Harris and the Chief Engineer were escaping from the impeller area where a great surge of foam and weed were trying to force its way through the perspex door.

The Doctor covered his ears as Victoria let out the most piercing scream. 'There! I knew you could do it . . . ' But as Victoria continued to scream frantically, the Doctor's relief soon diminished when he turned to see what she was screaming at. 'Oh dear,' he said. 'No wonder!'

With the foam and weed now threatening to burst through the perspex doors of the Impeller Area, engineers were rushing around the Hall in every direction. Harris called to two of them: 'All release valves open!'

'What are you doing, man?' yelled the Chairperson angrily as she and the Doctor joined Harris, who was directing operations from the control platform.

Harris turned sharply on her. 'I'm going to save the lives of an awful lot of people, Miss Jones.' He nervously flicked the lock of hair from his eye, then bellowed to another engineer. 'Close feed lines one to six!' The engineer nodded, then started turning a huge release valve gauge wheel.

The Chairperson protested. 'You mean – you're giving up? You're evacuating?'

'Open your eyes, Miss Jones!' snapped Harris, ignoring all respect for his superior. 'Can't you see what's happening? We're being strangled! I can't risk the lives of these men here any longer!'

The Doctor interrupted. 'Just another few minutes, Harris. That's all we need.'

'Doctor!' shouted Price from the Cone. 'We're ready with the scream!'

'Well, Harris?' pleaded the Doctor.

Another agonising decision for Harris. He sighed, rubbed the back of his head aimlessly, then turned back to the engineer. 'Hold the release valves!' The engineer stopped turning the huge gauge wheel. 'All right, Doctor,' warned Harris, 'you'd better be quick. What are you going to do?'

The Doctor immediately became very animated. 'Well, I

wired up all those loudspeakers there to the pipeline. The sound of Victoria's scream will be put through this . . . ' He delved into his pocket and brought out a small electronic gadget no bigger than a single microchip.

Harris was puzzled. 'What does that do?' he asked sceptically.

'It's an adaptable little toy of my own,' said the Doctor, leading Harris and the Chairperson back to the Cone. 'Together with the amplifiers, it should produce a sonic layer sound wave.'

'You mean, like a laser light beam?' suggested the Chairperson.

'More or less.' The Doctor inserted his gadget into the makeshift complex of wires behind the Cone. 'This sound should then travel through your speakers attached to the pipeline, and so through to the nerve centre of the weed colony.'

Harris still looked doubtful. 'Will that destroy the Weed here in the Refinery?'

The Doctor's head popped up from behind the Cone. 'Well – no. I'm afraid we shall have to do battle with that ourselves.'

'How?'

The Doctor moved to a line of speakers already wired up. 'We use these!'

Everyone, including Jamie and Victoria, hadn't the faintest idea what the Doctor was talking about. Their fears and doubts were further intensified when the pipeline tube above once again echoed to the deafening sound of the thumping heartbeat.

The Doctor now had to shout to be heard. 'Mr Price! If the foam and weed attack us, we merely aim these loudspeakers directly at them. Whatever you do, don't get in the way of any one of the speakers. The sonic sound waves would cut you to pieces!'

'Doctor!' Jamie was pointing in horror towards the huge central video monitor. The screen was showing a surge of

177

bubbling white foam, gushing its way down one of the long corridors leading to the Control Hall. And in that foam the heinous figure of a gigantic Weed Creature, its menacing tentacles flapping about in uncontrollable fury.

'It's making for the Hall!' yelled Harris. 'Chief! Follow me!'

Harris and the Chief Engineer rushed into the corridor to be met by the deafening squeals of not only the giant Weed Creature, but also its minions, the wriggling small clumps of weed, popping, and hissing gas in the surging foam. Harris shouted frantically, 'Back!' He and the Chief retreated back into the Control Hall.

'Full alert!' yelled Harris. 'Lock all doors!' As he spoke, Price flicked a switch and the emergency alarm klaxon horns echoed through the Refinery. The whole place was now thrown into a panic.

'The doors won't last much longer!' called Jamie. His eyes were firmly fixed towards the perspex doors of the impeller area, which were buckling under the weight of the foam and a second Weed Creature.

The Doctor grabbed hold of two passing engineers, and practically threw two loudspeakers at each of them. 'Take these and use them as weapons. Remember – don't point them at any human person!' The bewildered engineers took the speakers, and rushed off in different directions.

Harris's sudden shout was chilling and hysterical: '*Look Out!*'

There was a loud cracking sound as the door leading to the Compound Corridor burst open, and a great surge of foam gushed into the hall.

'Oh my God!' yelled the Chairperson. It was probably the only time she had ever shown emotion.

'Everybody back to the platform!' yelled Harris over the deafening sound of the shrieks and screams and thumping alien heartbeat. The Chairperson, Victoria, and some of the engineers made their way to the temporary safety of the raised control platform.

178

The Hall was now in total pandemonium as the aggressive foam surged ahead, swamping all and everyone in its path.

The Doctor went quickly to Price at the Cone. 'The tape recording, Price!' he yelled frantically. 'Turn it on, man!' But Price was paralysed with fear, staring in open-mouthed horror at the advancing wall of foam and the gradual approach of the hissing Weed Creature. The Doctor took hold of Price's shoulders and shook them firmly, shouting, 'Which switch is it, Price? Tell me!' Price suddenly snapped out of his state of shock. He looked at his feet. The foam was already swirling around his ankles. 'Turn on the recorder, Price. Do you hear me?' Without a word, Price slammed the switch down.

The Hall immediately echoed to the deafening sound of Victoria's screams, repeated over and over again with an electronic echo overlaid. Everyone clutched their ears in agony, for the screams were of such a high pitch that they were unbearable to listen to.

The wall of foam was now surging about the hall nearly waist-high. The Doctor, Jamie and Price struggled their way towards the raised control platform where the others were waiting with a line of loudspeakers. They were all virtually trapped into one small area of the Hall.

'Your speakers!' yelled the Doctor. 'Switch them on and aim them directly at the Weed!'

As he was speaking, the tentacles of the giant Weed Creature suddenly leapt out of the foam and snaked towards the group now sheltering on the raised platform. One of the tentacles reached out and curled itself around the Doctor's ankle. But Harris moved quickly, grabbed hold of the Doctor around his waist, and held on to him firmly.

'Do as I say!' yelled the Doctor again, struggling to free his ankle from the tentacles. 'Turn on the speakers – *now*!'

Every man on the platform who was holding a loud-speaker, turned it on, directing it straight at the Weed Creature. The sound that reverberated around the Hall was shattering. Victoria's recorded screams, overlaid on top of the existing ones, were deafening, terrifying. The helpless group looked on in fear and horror, waiting, hoping. But the weed and foam showed no sign of being affected by the Doctor's burst of electronic sound.

'It's not working!' shrieked the Chairperson. 'We can't hold it any longer!'

'Wait!' yelled the Doctor.

The sound of Victoria's recorded screams was growing in intensity. But the foam surged up the steps relentlessly, and the weed clumps wriggled and squealed and popped. Gradually, the Weed Creature itself moved closer and closer towards the raised platform, hissing gas fumes as it approached.

The Chairperson was coughing and spluttering. 'I tell you, it's not working!' she insisted, struggling to breathe. 'We're finished!'

'No!' Harris's voice boomed out above the recorded screams. 'Something's happening! Look at the Weed! Look at the foam!'

The Doctor suddenly felt a release of tension as the tentacle of the giant Weed Creature uncurled from around his ankle. Then he turned with the others to look at the amazing sight before them.

The bubbling white foam was retreating, not slowly, but rapidly. And as it did so, the noise it made was extraordinary, like the sound of wind rushing through a tunnel. But the most terrifying sight of all was the giant Weed Creature itself. Victoria's screams had clearly penetrated into its very soul, if the poor wretched fugitive from the deep possessed such a thing. Its squeals of agony were enough to chill the blood, and its tentacles flapped about helplessly in the air. Gradually, the huge shapeless mass withdrew towards the Compound door, taking with it the weed clumps that had nestled around it. After they had gone, all that was left were a few tiny blobs of bubbling white foam.

It took several moments for everyone in the Hall to realise that the battle against the Weed was over – and won. Finally, it was Price who led the engineers in a rousing cheer for the Doctor.

'Incredible!' proclaimed the Chairperson, clasping her hands together in ecstatic relief. 'Absolutely incredible!' She even found it possible to laugh at Perkins, her secretary. During the entire operation he had been crouched in a corner of the platform, shielded by Victoria. Soon, out of sheer relief, everyone was rocking with laughter.

'It worked!' said Harris incredulously. 'It actually worked!' And indeed there was no doubt about it. Not only was the Hall clear of weed and foam, but so too was the impeller area.

The Doctor picked himself up from the floor and called out, 'Everyone – turn off your speakers!' Victoria did so, and Price hurried back to the Cone to stop Victoria's screams on the recording machine.

The Hall was at last plunged into a peaceful silence.

'But what about the nerve centre of the weed out at the Control Rig?' asked Harris. 'D'you think we've destroyed it?'

The Doctor smiled. 'I think you should find out, Mr Harris.'

Harris nodded, and went to the Cone. 'Price. Send out one of the Company helicopters. I want a report from the Control Rig right away.' Price turned back to the control panel, and set about re-establishing contact with the outside world.

Within a few moments the Hall was bustling with activity again, as engineers quickly returned to their posts.

The Chairperson looked absolutely exhausted. But as she ran her fingers through her hair in an attempt to tidy it, one could sense that she was a far more vulnerable and attractive woman than she had ever revealed before. Nonetheless she was the first person to appreciate who was responsible for winning the seemingly hopeless battle against the Weed. 'I don't quite know what to say, Doctor,' she smiled, 'except – thank you.'

The Doctor smiled back. 'That is more than sufficient,' he replied. 'But I can assure you, the person we owe it all to is – Victoria.' He turned to look at Victoria, who had her back towards them nearby. She was in tears, sobbing deeply. 'Victoria!' The Doctor went to her quickly, and put a comforting arm around her shoulders. 'Victoria, my dear. What's the matter?'

Victoria looked up. Her face was pale and drawn. 'I . . . I was so frightened. I always am whenever . . . ' She broke down again. 'Oh, Doctor, I can't go on like this . . . I just can't . . . ' The Doctor held her in his arms, and exchanged a worried look over her shoulders with Jamie.

'Doctor!' Harris was calling from the Cone. 'They're safe!'

The Doctor left Jamie to look after Victoria, then hurried across to join Harris.

'Look at them! They're safe! We've won!' Harris was excitedly watching the huge central video screen. A group of people were shown there, gathered together in the Log Room of the Control Rig. Amongst them were Robson, Maggie Harris, van Lutyens, and Chief Baxter. But they were no longer the demented, half-human Weed Creatures the Doctor had last seen on the platform of the rig. The frond-like weed formations had disappeared from their necks and arms, the colour had returned to their faces, and although they still looked a little dazed, their eyes were bright and alert. Harris could hardly contain himself as he called out eagerly to the video screen. 'Maggie! Mr Robson! Can you hear me?'

Robson looked straight into the camera and replied. His voice was no longer a whisper. It came through loud and clear. 'Yes, Mr Harris, we can hear you.'

'Maggie, are you all right? The Weed – has it gone?'

The Doctor, Jamie and Victoria, the Chairperson, Harris, Perkins, Price, the Chief Engineer, everyone in the Control Hall was watching the video screen anxiously, waiting for Maggie's reply.

'Yes, Frank – it's gone. We're all perfectly safe.'

All around the Hall there were expressions of emotional relief.

'Just one question though,' continued Maggie. 'Would someone please tell me how the hell I got here!'

There was a momentary pause. Harris looked from the screen to the Doctor. He started to chuckle, then laugh. Price joined in, then the Chairperson, then Perkins. Soon, everyone in the Hall was rocking with uncontrollable laughter, a pure release of tension.

The mood quickly changed to loud cheers all round as the sound of the giant impeller was suddenly heard, throbbing with life again, echoing throughout the Refinery and the shores beyond.

The Doctor smiled gently, and looked up at the illuminated panel on top of the Cone. Every one of the rigs shown there was flashing with coloured lights.

Euro-Gas was back in business.

'I'd still like to know how I got out to that rig,' insisted Maggie, as she poured after-dinner coffee for her guests, who included Robson, the Doctor, Jamie, and Victoria. 'I mean, I can't even swim.'

'You can't remember anything at all?' asked her husband.

'Nothing. It was as though I'd had a nightmare, and had woken up in the middle of the North Sea!'

The Doctor smiled sympathetically. 'Nightmares can sometimes be a very strong emotional experience, Mrs Harris.'

'But how *did* I get out to that Rig?' asked Maggie.

'My guess is that you were cocooned by the foam, and quite literally, transported out there.'

Maggie shivered. 'How horrible!'

'Well, Harris, all I can say is, you were right,' said Robson, who had fully regained his robust appearance. 'I should've listened to you in the first place.'

Harris shook his head. 'I doubt it would've helped. As it

turned out, we were lucky we didn't tamper with that Weed.'

Everyone laughed as Maggie turned to her husband and said, 'And the next time you ask me to get something out of your desk, you can come and do it yourself!'

There was more laughter as Robson added, 'And to think I wanted to keep you locked up, Doctor. Just as well for us all that Harris here is inclined to disobey orders!' He dabbed his mouth with his napkin, then rose from the table. 'Well, that was a splendid dinner, Mrs Harris. Now, if you'll excuse me, I'm rather tired.'

'Of course,' said Maggie, rising from the table. Everyone but Victoria did likewise.

'Shall we see you in the morning, Doctor?' asked Robson.

The Doctor shook his head. 'I don't think so, Mr Robson. I'm afraid my friends and I must travel on.'

'Oh, really? Where are you going?'

The Doctor took a risky glance at Jamie. 'Er – well, we haven't quite made up our mind.'

'Even if we had,' complained Jamie, 'it wouldn't make any difference. We still wouldn't get there!' He grinned cheekily at the Doctor.

Robson smiled, a rare event for him. But he was clearly sorry to see the last of the Doctor and his companions. 'Well, if you're ever around these parts again, don't hesitate to drop in on us – only through the front gate next time, eh?'

Everyone laughed, then said their farewells to Controller Robson, who went off to resume the long career that meant so much to him.

The Doctor yawned and rubbed his eyes. 'I suppose it's about time we went too, eh, Jamie?' He turned to Victoria, who was still sitting at the table, her face resting on her hands. 'Are you ready, Victoria?'

Victoria slowly looked up at him. There were tears welling up in her eyes.

'Hey Victoria!' Jamie went to her immediately. 'What is it? What's the matter?'

Victoria looked away. She was too upset to answer.

The Doctor went and sat beside her. Taking her hand and patting it he said, in that soft, inimitably kind and understanding way that was so characteristic of him, 'It's all right, my dear. I know. You don't want to come with us, do you?'

Victoria found it impossible to look at the Doctor. 'I . . . I don't know. I don't want to leave you, but . . . ' Finally, she plucked up courage to look at him. 'How *did* you know?'

The Doctor smiled at her affectionately. 'I suspected it.'

'Would you mind?' she asked.

'Victoria!' protested Jamie. 'You can't!'

'Be quite, Jamie!' the Doctor said firmly. Then he turned back to Victoria. 'You want to stay, settle down?'

Victoria bit her lip nervously, nodded.

'Then if you really want to – you must do it.'

Victoria buried her head in his shoulder. 'Oh, Doctor,' she agonised, 'I'm so sorry . . . '

'It's all right, my dear . . . all right . . . ' He patted her gently on the back of the head, then turned to Maggie. 'Mrs Harris, would it be all right if Victoria stayed with you for a while. You see, she has no parents or family of her own, and . . . '

'Of course she can!' Maggie interrupted immediately. 'We'd be delighted to look after Victoria for as long as she likes to stay. Isn't that so, Frank?'

Harris nodded enthusiastically. 'With the greatest of pleasure!'

For the first time, Victoria's eyes lit up 'Oh, Mrs Harris, Mr Harris – would you really mind?'

Maggie responded by easing Victoria up from the table, and hugging her.

The Doctor looked relieved. He was concealing the personal sadness he felt. 'Thank you both – very much.' Then, for Victoria's sake, he quickly became very business-like. 'We'll stay here tonight, Victoria – just in case you want to think again . . . '

185

'Aye!' snapped Jamie resentfully. 'You're talking nonsense, Victoria – you know you are!'

'Jamie!' the Doctor reacted firmly. 'This is something Victoria must decide for herself. It's her life. We must not interfere.'

Victoria was watching Jamie closely. She couldn't bear that crumpled, hurt look on his face.

The windows of the Harrises' married quarters were thick with frost. But, thanks to an early morning shaft of sunlight which had not been forecast by the computers, the frost was now beginning to melt and trickle.

Inside the kitchen, someone was rubbing a small clear patch on the window. Victoria's face peered out. It was clear she hadn't slept well that night, for her eyes were puffed up from crying. In the distance, she could just pick out the small, stocky figure of Jamie, winding his way in the cold through the grounds of the Refinery Compound. As soon as she caught sight of him, she felt a sinking, hollow feeling in her stomach. Jamie was the best friend she ever had, or was every likely to have. Even though at times he was pompous and opinionated, she knew only too well how difficult it was going to be to continue her life without him.

'There he is,' she thought, as she went out to meet Jamie on the kitchen patio, 'that funny little figure in his kilt, pullover, and tam-o-shanter.' In a few hours time, she would never see him again.

'You're up early,' he said awkwardly. 'Didn't you sleep?'

'Oh – yes,' Victoria flustered. 'I'm feeling fine.'

'Good.' There was an unnatural pause between them, until Jamie finally said, 'D'you know what the Doctor's done?'

'No?'

'He's only gone down to the beach! He gets worse every day!' He laughed falsely. But Victoria had difficulty in even raising a smile. There was another awkward pause, and then Jamie could contain himself no longer. 'You're still not sure, are you?'

'Yes, I'm sure now,' replied Victoria decisively, 'but that doesn't make it any easier leaving you and the Doctor.'

'Aye. We've been together a good time now. Has the Doctor said anything else to you?'

'No. You know him – he wouldn't. He believes in people making up their own minds.'

'Aye.' Jamie lowered his eyes and made aimless patterns with his foot in the frost. 'You'll be happy here?'

'I think so. The Harrises are nice people.'

'I know. But they're not from your time, are they?'

Victoria was finding it incredibly difficult to explain how she really felt. 'The thing is, I wouldn't be at ease back in Victorian times anyway. After all, I've no family left there.'

'Aye, I know,' sighed Jamie. 'Ah, well . . . ' He turned to leave.

'Jamie!' Victoria quickly stopped him. 'You wouldn't go without – well, saying goodbye, would you?'

'Och, no! Of course not!'

Victoria sighed with relief. 'Good.'

'Victoria . . . ' Jamie turned back as though there was something he just had to say to her.

'Yes?'

'I . . . I . . . ' he stammered.

'Yes, Jamie?'

Jamie's courage failed. 'Oh . . . nothing. See you later.' He turned, and quickly made his way back towards the beach.

A short time later, the Doctor said their farewells to Victoria, and left her with Maggie and Harris on the beach. It was a strange parting, one that seemed totally unnecessary and unnatural to Jamie.

The sky was now a clear blue, and the sun was streaming down on the TARDIS which was waiting at the far end of the beach, covered in a thin film of melting frost.

As the Doctor and Jamie made their way along the beach, they stopped just once to turn and wave back to the solitary trio who were watching them from the distance. Jamie's face had that crumpled, upset look about it again, so the Doctor quickly took him by the arm and led him off.

Victoria watched the Doctor and Jamie disappear inside the TARDIS. It seemed unnatural to her too, the fact that she was not going with them, and large tears began to roll down her cherry-red cheeks.

The grunting, grinding sound of the TARDIS filled the air. Victoria shivered with the cold, then turned to look anxiously at Maggie and Harris. They responded by smiling at her reassuringly.

'We can't just . . . leave her,' begged Jamie, as he and the Doctor stared sadly at the three figures they had just left behind on the beach. But this time they were watching them on the scanner inside the TARDIS.

'We're not leaving her, Jamie,' sighed the Doctor. 'It was Victoria's decision to stay.'

'Aye.'

'Don't worry about her,' said the Doctor trying to sound confident. 'She'll be happy with the Harrises.'

'Och, I'm not worrying!' replied Jamie unconvincingly. 'Come on, let's go!'

'All right.' The Doctor turned back to the Control Unit. 'Where would you like to go?'

'I couldna' care less!' Although he tried to resist it, Jamie's eyes were still rivetted to the scanner.

The Doctor watched him for a moment, smiling affectionately at his young companion's emotional outburst. He knew just how much Jamie was going to miss Victoria. 'You know, Jamie,' he said, 'I was fond of her too . . . '

He sighed again, turned back to the controls and flicked all the necessary switches that immediately set the TARDIS in motion.

The grinding and grunting sound of the dematerialising TARDIS gradually disappeared. And in its place, the seabirds returned, swooping low over the surface of the water, searching out the fish they had thought they would never see again.

Out and beyond was the vast expanse of sea. The cruel, unyielding sea. Calm again now. The fury gone.

All that remained were the small blobs of bubbling white foam and straggling clumps of seaweed that rolled gently over the waves of the incoming tide.

DOCTOR WHO

0426114558	TERRANCE DICKS **Doctor Who and The Abominable Snowmen**	£1.35
0426200373	**Doctor Who and The Android Invasion**	£1.25
0426201086	**Doctor Who and The Androids of Tara**	£1.35
0426116313	IAN MARTER **Doctor Who and The Ark in Space**	£1.35
0426201043	TERRANCE DICKS **Doctor Who and The Armageddon Factor**	£1.50
0426112954	**Doctor Who and The Auton Invasion**	£1.50
0426116747	**Doctor Who and The Brain of Morbius**	£1.35
0426110250	**Doctor Who and The Carnival of Monsters**	£1.35
042611471X	MALCOLM HULKE **Doctor Who and The Cave Monsters**	£1.50
0426117034	TERRANCE DICKS **Doctor Who and The Claws of Axos**	£1.35
042620123X	DAVID FISHER **Doctor Who and The Creature from the Pit**	£1.35
0426113160	DAVID WHITAKER **Doctor Who and The Crusaders**	£1.50
0426200616	BRIAN HAYLES **Doctor Who and The Curse of Peladon**	£1.50
0426114639	GERRY DAVIS **Doctor Who and The Cybermen**	£1.50
0426113322	BARRY LETTS **Doctor Who and The Daemons**	£1.50

Prices are subject to alteration

DOCTOR WHO

0426101103	DAVID WHITAKER **Doctor Who and The Daleks**	£1.50
042611244X	TERRANCE DICKS **Doctor Who and The Dalek Invasion of Earth**	£1.50
0426103807	**Doctor Who and The Day of the Daleks**	£1.35
042620042X	**Doctor Who – Death to the Daleks**	£1.35
0426119657	**Doctor Who and The Deadly Assassin**	£1.50
0426200969	**Doctor Who and The Destiny of the Daleks**	£1.35
0426108744	MALCOLM HULKE **Doctor Who and The Dinosaur Invasion**	£1.35
0426103726	**Doctor Who and The Doomsday Weapon**	£1.50
0426201464	IAN MARTER **Doctor Who and The Enemy of the World**	£1.50
0426200063	TERRANCE DICKS **Doctor Who and The Face of Evil**	£1.50
0426201507	ANDREW SMITH **Doctor Who – Full Circle**	£1.50
0426112601	TERRANCE DICKS **Doctor Who and The Genesis of the Daleks**	£1.35
0426112792	**Doctor Who and The Giant Robot**	£1.35
0426115430	MALCOLM HULKE **Doctor Who and The Green Death**	£1.35

Prices are subject to alteration

THIS OFFER EXCLUSIVE TO

READERS

**Pin up magnificent full colour posters of
DOCTOR WHO**

**Just send £2.50 for the first poster and £1.25
for each additional poster**

TO: PUBLICITY DEPARTMENT *
W. H. ALLEN & CO PLC
44 HILL STREET
LONDON W1X 8LB

Cheques, Postal Orders made payable to WH Allen PLC

POSTER 1 ☐	**POSTER 2** ☐	**POSTER 3** ☐
POSTER 4 ☐	**POSTER 5** ☐	

Please allow 28 DAYS for delivery.

I enclose £ _____

CHEQUE NO. _____

ACCESS, VISA CARD NO. _____

Name _____

Address _____

_____

_____

***For Australia, New Zealand, USA and Canada apply to distributors
listed on back cover for details and local price list**

FANTASTIC

POSTER OFFERS!

1

2

3

4

5

In the dark uncharted depths of the North Sea
it has lurked, growing in strength, growing in
size, and striking terror into the hearts of
mariners down the untold centuries.

Landing near a North Sea gas refinery off the
east coast of England, the TARDIS crew are
immediately accused of sabotage. Several rig
crews have mysteriously vanished, strange
pressure build-ups have been detected, and in
the refinery's pipelines the Doctor can hear the
steady, rhythmic beat of — what?

Soon the Doctor, Jamie and Victoria will find
themselves at the unrelenting mercy of the
deadliest and most terrifying foe they have
ever encountered . . .

Disbributed by

USA: LYLE STUART INC, 120 Enterprise Ave, Secaucus, New Jersey 07094
CANADA: CANCOAST BOOKS, 90 Signet Drive, Unit 3, Weston, Ontario M9L 1T5
AUSTRALIA: GORDON AND GOTCH LTD *NEW ZEALAND*: GORDON AND GOTCH (NZ) L

ISBN 0-426-20259-7

UK:£1.95   USA:$3.50
CANADA:$4.95 NZ:$8.95
Science fiction/TV Tie-in

9 780426 202592